IGNITED

MAYA DANIELS

IGNITED

MAYA DANIELS

VIPER
BOOKS

By Maya Daniels

Daywalker Series

Investigated

Infiltrated

Instigated

Initiated

Infuriated

Ignited

Vinci Books

vinci-books.com

Published by Vinci Books Ltd in 2026

1

A CIP catalogue record for this book is available from the British Library.
Paperback ISBN: 9781036706777

The EU GPSR authorised representative is Logos Europe, 9 rue Nicolas Poussion, 17000 La Rochelle, France
contact@logoseurope.eu

Chapter One

When things go from bad to worse, expecting a horrible scenario in which the Fates will take advantage and kick you while you're down is kind of a given. Being brought to your knees too many times to count is never enough, be it as a human or a supernatural. In this it seems we have too much in common with our very mortal cohabitants in this world. It's been a constant occurrence in my life, so why fool myself otherwise? With that in mind, I stick to my proven method of distracting myself. In this case, it's not turning into a couch potato and stuffing my face with chocolate and food until I wind up in a coma.

To some, the chirping of birds, gurgling springs, or even soft whispers of the wind through the trees may be sounds that will relax them and bring a smile to their face. To others, like myself, the pained groan when Zoltan's body hits the floor after I sweep his feet under him is something that makes my heart sing.

A grin stretches my lips so high my cheeks hurt from it.

"Better." Huffing arrogantly like he didn't just eat the dust off the floor, he jumps on his feet.

"Better?" Slamming both fists on my hips, I glare at him. "You mean, 'that was awesome Franky. I absolutely did not see it coming.'"

"Calm down. You need to stop being cocky." Typical Zoltan, he is oblivious to the hole he is digging for himself. Who in their right mind will tell a female to calm down when there is steam coming out of her ears? A male, that's who. "Of course I saw it coming, I was just hoping that you would follow through and make sure I didn't get up. At the moment I could attack you right back, and then you've wasted all your energy for just one solid hit."

"You want me to kill you?"

"I need you to stop holding back, Francesca."

"It doesn't work that way, you jerk. You are helping me gain more control. Me making you bleed or hurting you doesn't show control at all. It just means I go all nuts again."

"I am immortal, so if it takes me bleeding to ensure I won't be worried about you when the time comes, I'm willing to have my blood spilled. Stop holding back." The words are punctuated with a stubborn tilt of his chin.

From the very beginning, Zoltan has been adamant about making sure I'm trained properly to face whatever Roberti throws at us—or anyone else for that matter. That damn bond turned him into an unbearable creature breathing down my neck and constantly pushing me harder. The difference with then and now is simple: he has stopped flirting, and he's no longer his arrogant self. Even the perpetual smirk is missing from his lips. Clinging to whatever tunnel vision that has him stuck in his head, he is hell bent on me training daily until I can barely twitch a finger. By the time we are through, I want to crawl back to my room. Eyeing him through slanted lids, my stomach somersaults when the realization hits me like a brick. It's right there in the hard set of his jaw, the clenching of his fists, and the stiff set of his shoulders. How have I never noticed it before?

He is afraid.

For me …

"Where is this coming from, Zoltan?" With my heart drumming against my ribcage, I take a step closer and reach for his face. The sharp lines of his firmly pressed lips and clenched jaw soften as he nuzzles his face in my palm. "This past week, I can't remember the last time you've pissed me off with your smirking. From the time I wake up until I pass out on the pillow from exhaustion, you are like a machine with just one setting. Tiring me to death is your mission in life."

Zoltan's lips part in a sigh and his stiff shoulders slump slightly, while his gaze searches my face. I wait him out, not daring to twitch a muscle while my heart is trying to punch a hole in my throat. It's unnerving seeing him afraid. He was calm and unperturbed when hunters had poisoned blades under his throat. I realize I'm counting on him always being like that, being my rock when everything around me is falling apart. When he starts lowering his mouth closer to mine, my face tilts up on its own, like a flower searching for the sun. I can feel his breath tickling my lips and it sends a frenzy of butterflies through my stomach.

"I can try to train with her if it'll be easier."

Jerking away from Zoltan, my head snaps to Soren. Leaning a shoulder on the wall with one ankle crossed over the other, he has been watching us like some creep for who knows how long. His silky pants shimmer like liquid silver down his legs where his bare feet poke out under them. And

3

would it kill him to put on a damn shirt? Platinum hair frames his perfect face with lips curled slightly at the edges, making him look like he knows something we don't. His golden eyes twinkle full of mischief while reflecting the flames flickering around the room.

The Dragon Blood is as sneaky as a freaking cat, catching us all unaware. You never know when he is going to pop up out of nowhere. I stifle my frustration so I don't hurt his feelings, but Zoltan doesn't suffer from being nice like that. The Daywalker turns his overwhelming glare at the object of his anger, his emotions descending over the three of us like a dark cloud. The training room is large enough to fit an army of us in it at the same time, yet all the oxygen gets sucked out like we are being vacuum sealed.

"I thought I should offer." Lifting both hands palms up, Soren looks as innocent as a child, though his voice echoing through the almost-empty space and bouncing off the walls all seductive-like and full of humor suggests otherwise.

"That's nice of you." Elbowing Zoltan until I hear him grunt, I smile tightly at Soren.

"He will continue taking advantage of your kindness, Francesca. How is it you can't see that?" Stepping slightly in front of me, Zoltan doesn't look away from the ancient Fae. For a moment, it's almost as if he is staring at the enemy.

"He can hear you." Hissing at his back, I poke him for emphasis. "It's time to take a break anyway." Speaking much louder, I sidestep the territorial vampire and head for Soren, wincing when all my muscles protest at the movement.

I can feel Zoltan's heat at my back.

"How are things going with the others?" When I'm a foot away from the Dragon Blood, a shiver crawls up my spine when Zoltan's shadow falls over Soren and sharpens his high cheekbones. "Are they acclimating to their powers yet? When can we see them?" The intent, unreadable look in his eyes makes me blabber like a fool.

"Meh, they are being childish." Flicking his wrist as if he's chasing flies, his lips twist with displeasure. "They keep fighting fate. No one wins against it, it just makes everyone miserable. What is the saying?" Tilting his head left and right, he snaps his fingers with a broad smile. "If you can't beat them, join them. That is all they need to do."

Unable to help myself, I smile right back at him. "Look at you picking up all the modern sayings. Soon enough you'll start saying dude." A giggle escapes me at the humor dancing in the ancient Fae's eyes.

"Did I do well?" The simple question is so full of eagerness that the smile slips from my lips.

"What?"

"Isn't that what you want, Francesca?" My confusion must be clear because a line forms between his perfect brows puckering them up. "For me to fit in the modern times, your time. Is that not what you want?"

The short hairs on the back of my neck stand on end when a feral growl comes from deep in Zoltan's chest.

"No." Flinching when I snap at him, I blow out a breath, my hands clenching at my sides. "It's not what I want, Soren. It's what *you* want. That's what you should do."

"Is it?" New interest sparkles in his gaze. He is totally ignoring Zoltan's presence and all his focus is centered on me. "I believe you want me to fit in with the rest of them. You are uneasy when I'm being myself."

"I'm uneasy when you are being creepy as fuck, like right now for example." A nervous laugh is pushed through my lips and I subtly slide to my right, blocking Zoltan from snatching the Fae by the throat. "And stop provoking Zoltan. It's annoying."

"I do no such thing, I assure you." The cheeky smile says he is doing exactly that and enjoying the crap out if it, too. "The mighty Zoltan is just unsure how to deal with his own emotions, as well as how to keep a female like you by his side. I'm not the only one that needs to come to terms with modern times, it seems."

A fist zooms past my head, ruffling the short hairs that have escaped my braid. I jump back a step when Zoltan's hand punches a hole through the wall an inch from Soren's face. The Fae doesn't bat an eye at the aggressive display, but I'm fighting a panic attack while I try to swallow my heart from my throat so it pushes back to my chest. It's beating wildly at the roof of my mouth and my eyes are about to pop out of their sockets. The vampire's body is vibrating and growing in front of me, his shoulders bunching and his muscles jumping. Zoltan's powers are blasting out as if I have placed my face in front of a fire, and my eyes tear up from the stinging of my skin, though it takes my brain a long moment to come online.

"Knock it off, both of you." Stepping between them like a referee, I slap a hand on each of their chests to separate them. "We have enough shit to deal with already. The last thing we need is to be biting each other's heads off."

A deep rumble followed by a predatory cry comes from the open doorway, freezing the blood in my veins. Tenebris bares his sharp teeth at both males, his tail lashing behind him in agitation. With his ears pinned to the back of his head, he glowers at them while his whiskers tremble on his curled upper lip. With paws as wide as my head, he pads closer until he reaches me and presses the left one on top of my foot. The action is loud and clear, a dare for them to continue messing with me and they'll both end up with his jaw clamped around their neck.

My hand grabs hold of the fur on his neck on instinct, my fingers sinking into the smooth, silky strands. As always, Tenebris rubs his cheek on my thigh, acknowledging the weird connection we formed what feels like a lifetime ago. From the first time I saw him, he hasn't left my side if he can help it.

"You are right, young dragon." Inclining his head regally, Soren straightens and pushes off the wall. "I apologize for causing you distress. It's all just good fun for me. I see now that I was mistaken."

Narrowing my eyes at his face, I say nothing. If I've learned anything about Soren, it's that he is always up to no good. Causing trouble like a toddler set loose in a toy store, the ancient Fae loves playing games with all of us. It's not like I'm special, either, because he does the same to all of my friends, too.

"I mean it, Soren." Stabbing my forefinger to the center of his chest, I emphasize each word with a new poke. "Stop. Making. Trouble."

"As you wish." The fond smile on his face makes me feel like an ass. I push the feeling away because I know it's just one of his ways to get what he wants.

Damn manipulative Fae.

"And what's wrong with you?" I turn to Tenebris when he starts nudging me with his whole body, guiding me forcefully toward the door.

An angry hiss is the answer to my glare.

"Let's see what made him come get you." Taking hold of my hand, Zoltan doesn't wait for and answer, nor does he hesitate for the Dragon Blood we are leaving behind. I have to walk faster to keep up with his pace.

"Would it be too much to ask for one day without any drama in this place?" Huffing, I look over my shoulder to see Soren following behind us at a slower pace. "Well, come on. No need to stay away from us, just don't be an ass."

"I shall try, dràgon òg." Closing the space between us, Soren's musical lilt when he speaks the ancient language spreads warmth through my chest.

He looks too willing to do what he is being told.

It doesn't sit well with me, but I let Zoltan guide me through the hallways anyways as we follow Tenebris to whatever needs our attention. There is an insistent feeling at the back of my mind that a shitstorm is coming, but I can't really put my finger on it. Once again, I glance at Soren over my shoulder.

If I learned one thing for sure, it's that when a Fae is willing to play by your rules, you better start reading the fine print real fast.

Chapter Two

"Will you stop staring?" Zoltan murmurs from behind me, looming over my shoulders while I lean on the wall stretching my neck like a giraffe to get a better look.

"You can't be serious. Did you see him?" Whisper-yelling, I don't even turn to give him *THE* look. "What in all the worlds happened to him?"

Fenrir and Leo are leaning close to each other face to face, whispering low enough that if not for staring at their lips and seeing them move, I may think they're about to kiss. It looks hot as fuck, but that's not what I'm supposed to be paying attention to. It's not why I'm glued to the wall impersonating Soren the creep.

No, It's Fenrir.

The illusion that makes the Fae who he is, or as I know him mostly, is gone. No more androgynous face, or platinum blonde hair. Even the vibe coming off him is no longer soft, calm, and collected. Instead, sharp features with cheekbones that will cut through stone are framed by a curtain of midnight black hair reaching down to his waist, shining like oil under the flickering flames and the streaming moonlight coming through the windows.

Deep red runes form thin lines pulsing softly across his jaw, forehead, and neck, disappearing under the collar of his black t-shirt. He doesn't look like the male I know. Not like the one I called friend in any case. And it's not so much his changed appearance that freaks the hell out of me, and obviously Tenebris too since he brought us here to show me this. It's the energy coming from Fenrir and the way he holds himself.

He looks primal.

Scary even.

"You think Roberti got to him and messed him up?" Glancing at Zoltan is a bad idea.

My self-appointed babysitter is giving me a cocked-eyebrow look, calling me insane without opening his mouth. Not wanting to talk in case I'm overheard, I wave my hand in the direction of the two males who are conversing silently but just a little too enthusiastically, fast enough to make my wrist pop like a firecracker in the silent hallway.

My heart stops.

So did everyone else's, including the two I am spying on.

"Oh hey." Acting like I'm coincidently coming from around the corner, I grin at Fenrir and Leo, pretending I just noticed them. "You have to help me and keep Zoltan away from me. He is trying to kill me with his training. Did you hear that pop? That was from my joints and all thanks to the jerk." For some stupid reason I keep spewing words. Probably because I'm a moron and completely unable to close my mouth to stop the disaster I can clearly see coming. "How are you doing, pup? Hanging in there, huh? Oh, hey Fenrir, long time no see." To my horror, I giggle too, which makes both of them squint at me.

"You should stop. Honestly, it would actually be painful to watch you continue." Leo grins at my stupidity, and I cringe seeing the laughter he is suppressing.

"I don't know what you're talking about." Giving it a last-ditch effort, I even try to look confused.

Even Zoltan chuckles at that.

I glare at him since he has decided to stand far enough away that I can't elbow him.

The vampire is learning my tricks.

"I believe he is referring to your spying skills, dràgon òg," Soren ever-the-helpful chirps from behind me, and I grind my teeth at his words.

At this, Fenrir's lips twitch at the corners, although the haunted look in his white-on-black eyes takes my breath away. My ribs tighten painfully and prevent me from taking a full breath. I haven't seen the Fae since Leo, Daren, and Astara took over the Order of the Academy. What I'm looking at now is an entirely different person, and there's no trace of my friend and confidante.

"Fenrir …" my voice trails off when he lifts a hand to stop me from saying anything else.

"It's a long story." Soren snorts indignantly at Fenrir's comment from behind me, but the Fae ignores him. "And I will explain everything when I can. Right now, I need Leo's help and a promise from all of you that whoever comes back with him to Sienna will be protected."

"Human?" Zoltan turns all business, his arms folding across his chest in reaction to an unknown threat to what he considers his domain. If he keeps this territorial bullshit up, I honestly won't be surprised if he starts pissing on everything.

"Half bloods …" My spine snaps to attention hearing that. "I can't be sure how many will be coming, but some might be just like the mother and two half bloods that Leo brought not long ago." Running a hand through his hair in frustration, Fenrir huffs out a heavy sigh. "Myst made a deal with a human to have them saved from the hunter's compounds."

"And we trust this human?" I really want to punch Zoltan for the question, because as soon as I hear half bloods, I want to run head first and get them out myself. I understand his worry too, so I bite on the inside of my mouth to keep it shut.

"I do." My body jerks as if Fenrir has slapped me.

"You trust humans?" I couldn't keep quiet any longer. Out of all of us, Fenrir is the one who looks down his nose at everyone, including some supernaturals.

"I trust that human. Not *humans*, Drake."

"Oh, we are back to Drake now. Got it." For some reason it rubs me wrong that he is distancing himself. I've done nothing to deserve it, which makes it an even more bitter pill to swallow. "Anyway"—Cutting off whatever he was going to say to that, I turn to Leo—"what can we do to help?"

"Nothing now until we know more about this. I will go meet with the human first." Scrubbing at the back of his neck, Leo peers at Zoltan with his lips pressed in a firm line. "You okay with that? I don't think I have the strength right now to deal with newcomers while I keep trying to control the influx of powers that continue to hit me from the academy and having to worry about fighting you if it comes to that."

"Why would he fight you?" Frowning I turn from Leo to Zoltan. "Why would you fight him?"

"He allowed himself a full transformation," Soren answers, while a muscle keeps pulsing in Zoltan's clenched jaw. "The territorial instincts are still too strong and he can't keep them under control. Not yet. It's what happens when you ignore or refuse your nature for too long." My eyes follow Soren's hand when he reaches up and rubs at the center of his chest absentmindedly. "Isn't that correct, Rìgh fuil?"

"What did you call him?" I have to remind myself that Soren can snap my neck with a flick of his wrist, otherwise I may slap him for constantly speaking in tongues.

"Blood King." An intent gleam enters Soren's gaze while he stares at Zoltan, as if he's daring him to dispute him or say something to contradict him. "Isn't that what you are, Zoltan?"

"We will take anyone the human brings to the portal and protect them." Turning his back to the Dragon Blood, Zoltan answers Leo. He is a bigger person than me. If looks can kill, Soren would be ashes right now based on the glare I pin him with. "As long as Francesca is nowhere near them, you will have no problem with me. Just keep them out of sight for now."

"I can help protect them, too." Jumping in their conversation, I lean heavily on Tenebris so I can see around Zoltan. "Wouldn't they be safer here with all of us? Let's not forget we still don't know if we have more moles telling Roberti our every move."

"As much as I would love to fight beside you, Drake, and antagonize Zoltan every chance I get at the same time, I don't think that's a smart idea. Not right now." One side of Leo's mouth curls, and it softens the sting of his words. It doesn't feel nice to be excluded.

"The two of you should talk," Fenrir says almost under his breath while he darts glances at Soren. "Don't do what I did." His white-on-black eyes lock on Zoltan and some unspoken understanding flows between them.

I want to ask a hundred questions but keep quiet, diverting my attention from them by gliding a hand over the panther's back. A deep purr vibrates through my palm all the way up to my elbow, and I look down at Tenebris. His keen, bright green eyes flick between all of us, his intelligence and cunning raising goosebumps over my arms.

"I must go back across the portal." Fenrir rolls his shoulders as if uncomfortable for being here with us. "If you need me, I will come … if I can. Do not hold it against me if I'm otherwise occupied."

"Your loyalty has never been a question, old friend." Clasping the Fae's forearm, Zoltan slaps him on the back. "Do what you need to do. If you need our help, all you have to do is ask."

"This feels like a goodbye." Panic surges through me and I snatch Fenrir's arm in a tight grip, my nails digging into his skin. "Why does this feel like a goodbye? Is it me? Did I make you not want to be here?"

Old triggers rear their ugly head, choking me. *Half blood, unworthy, abomination, unwanted … not enough, not enough, not enough …* Words scream on repeat in my mind and silence everything else.

"Franky." I snap out of my downward spiral when Fenrir shakes me by the shoulders hard enough to make Tenebris snap his jaws a hairsbreadth away from his hand in warning. "You are not at fault for anything. Myst needs me, and I have denied myself long enough what I knew in my heart to be true."

"Oh …" Blinking stupidly at him, I have to wait for the panic to subside so I can speak. Seeing Zoltan forcibly keeping himself from throwing the Fae off me clears the doubts that were trying to choke me as well. "I knew there was something between the two of you." Happiness warms my insides and I give Fenrir a big smile. "I'm not gonna say I won't miss having you around, Fenrir. I'll have no one to pick on."

Leo clears his throat loudly and my smile wobbles.

"The mutt will have to deal with all my glorious attitude now." If I'm blinking fast, it has nothing to do with the prickling tears at the back of my eyes. It's from the flickering flames. Right, that's the reason for sure.

"You cannot leave." There is no argument left when Soren speaks from behind me. "You made an oath."

"And you'll watch me break it, seann dràgon." Squaring his shoulders, the Fae glowers at Soren. "You can try to stop me, but I will not let you kill me easy."

"No one is killing anyone." Whirling on Soren, I grab his upper arm and shake him as if that will make him to stop being a jerk. He doesn't move an inch, but his eyes snap to my hand that is wrapped around his bicep. "You said it yourself: no one wins against the Fates. Stop being an ass or I'll castrate you."

I see Leo wince from the corner of my eye and Zoltan's eyebrows crawl up his forehead.

"Go, Fenrir. Say hi to Myst for me." Not taking my gaze away from Soren, I swallow the lump in my throat. "And don't be a stranger, okay?"

Not caring about the angry Dragon Blood, Fenrir turns me and wraps me up in a bone crushing hug. I cling to his shirt, grinding my teeth to stop the sob that's trying to escape me. With a kiss pressed on my forehead, he takes one step, then another before he spins on his heel and walks away. I keep looking at his back until it disappears out of sight.

"I'll come if you need me." Calling after him, my voice echoes off the high walls and ceilings.

"I know." I can hear him answer, but I wonder if I am just imagining it.

"He will be back." Zoltan comes behind me, his body enveloping mind as I lean the back of my head to his chest.

"Why is it that I don't believe you?"

He doesn't answer, and I'm grateful he is not trying to lie to me. There was a finality in Fenrir's hug that squeezed my heart until it felt like it would explode. I've always been on my own, even when Daren acted like he was there for me. Fenrir was the first true friend I had and watching him walk away feels like something inside me is breaking with no hope of repair. A chill spreads through me making me shiver in Zoltan's arms. Not even the heat of his body can warm me.

"It's the oath being broken," Soren spits in disgust.

"Huh?" My mind reeling, I turn absentmindedly toward him.

"That emptiness and ice you feel." His face twisted in anger, the Dragon Blood glares at the place where Fenrir disappeared. "It's the oath being broken."

"And you know this how?" Bile burns the back of my throat.

"He bound the two of you with the oath, and he can feel it break, too," Zoltan murmurs in my hair as he presses a kiss to the top of my head.

"I have no idea what any of you are talking about."

"It's time we have a talk." Zoltan sounds calm, but his heart is trying to punch a hole through his chest and my back.

"I will come for this talk as well." Soren juts his chin stubbornly.

I say nothing, still feeling raw from the knowledge that Fenrir left us for good. Zoltan tucks me under his arm, nodding at Leo as we walk past him. The alpha squeezes my arm in comfort but releases it too soon for my liking, and then we are gone.

I wish I can say the same about the ancient Dragon Blood following right behind me.

Soren is proving to be a bigger problem than I ever anticipated.

Chapter Three

People were giving us wary looks and a wide berth until we reached the dining hall. Not even the memory of my brother's head rolling on the floor stopped my feet from moving as Zoltan guided me to the corner of the large space we somehow marked as our own since the day I walked through those cursed gates of the academy. It feels like that was a different time.

A different life.

Placing me on one of the armchairs, the vampire arranged my limbs to make me comfortable. Feeling numb inside and not caring one way or the other, I let him do what he wants. As soon as Zoltan steps away and perches on the sofa closest to me, Tenebris plops over my feet, covering them with his body. That left Soren to situate himself across from me on another armchair. The ancient Fae grumbled something but took his seat.

"Dearly beloveds, we are gathered here today ..." I speak clearly before hysterical laughter bursts out of me. It really does feel like a funeral.

Soren gives me a worried look before his gaze darts to Zoltan.

"It's the breaking of the oath making you feel like that." He repeats Soren's words, taking a hold of my hand and rubbing my fingers between his.

"How is that possible, Zoltan? I don't remember taking or giving an oath to Soren, or Fenrir for that matter." I realize that I'm pressing the fingers of my free hand at the center of my chest, so I drop my hand limply in my lap. "It feels like I have an organ missing or something."

"You would not remember it because it was given at the time you were born." Soren clears his throat, leaning on the armchair like he is posing for a photoshoot. "Your father gave the oath in your name."

"Maybe you should join my father so you two can discuss it, then." If my father was alive, I think I might kill him myself right now. "What was it? Some deal, like an arranged marriage or whatever you want to call it?"

"We are not human." My palm started itching to slap the arrogant look off Soren's face.

Letting my fangs drop—as tiny as they are—and my eyes shift to the snake ones—or dragon vertical pupils as nature has made them—I grin humorlessly at the ancient Fae. "You don't say."

"Magnificent." Eagerly leaning his body forward, the awe on Soren's face made my stomach churn.

"The oath, Soren." Hissing to snap him out of whatever fantasy he is creating in his head, I tighten my hold on Zoltan's hand. "How do I get rid of this feeling. Fenrir was my friend … is my friend," I amend. "As much as I'll miss his stick-up-the-ass self around here, I shouldn't feel like a part of me is missing. This is not normal."

"You are the last of your kind." A glow enters his

orange eyes, which sends a shiver crawling up and down my numb body. "That oath was the right thing to do, and it has made it so your line will continue."

A yelp bursts out of me when Zoltan's hand clamps over mine like a metal vice, grinding my bones.

His face is carved out of stone, but he says nothing.

"Meaning what exactly?" Tugging on Zoltan's arm, I untangle my fingers from his and take his hand in both of mine. Touching him grounds me because it feels like the floor is about to fall from under my feet. "No more riddles. Speak plainly so there aren't any more misunderstandings. How am I the last of my kind? What about you?"

"The last female Dragon Blood, Francesca Drake." Eyelids lowering, Soren's calculating gaze sends alarms blaring through my brain. "It was my belief that you would need a strong royal Fae bloodline to continue yours. Fenrir was willing to take the oath, and until now, he saw it as an honor."

I laugh.

Peals of laughter shake my shoulders and tears gather around my lashes. The longer Soren stares at me like I've finally lost it, the louder I get. A stich forms on my side when I start gasping for air. Poor Zoltan looks ready to jump and kill something, lost as to how to deal with me right now.

"Oh, dear Fates, you are serious." Gulping air to fill up my lungs, a few more barks of laughter pass my lips. "You are kinda forgetting the most important thing in your idiotic plan, I think." Slowly and purposely, I point a finger at myself as if he is stupid. "Half blood. Repeat after me … half blood."

"You are a Dragon blood." Straightening his spine, Soren looks like I just insulted him. "Your bloodline is strong enough for an offspring. You will continue your line."

"That was your and my father's idea? To force Fenrir into an oath? And then what? When I'm old enough I'll jump right in and start popping out babies?" I realize that I actually feel sorry for Soren. He is delusional. "This right here"—Swirling a hand at my lap indicating my uterus, I glare at him—"does not work. You can't be that far gone not to understand that. We can't breed; it's scientifically proven, in case you missed the memo."

I don't bother mentioning that's why Zoltan and I have been humping like rabbits every chance we get without me batting an eye. As a half blood, I can't have younglings. I knew that since I learned what being a half-blood meant. So did Zoltan, at least that is what I assumed. Uneasiness clamps my stomach and I dare a glance at his face.

I wish he looks angry.

The blank expression he is wearing spikes my blood pressure through the roof. The slow smile curling Soren's lips makes the dining hall spin around, so I grab hold of the armchair in a white-knuckled grip. My chest starts rising and falling rapidly, all the oxygen in the room not enough to help me breathe. Dark spots dance at the corners of my eyes, so I don't fight Zoltan when his hand takes my head and pushes it between my knees.

"Slow breaths." His voice sounds from very far away and is muffled by the thundering of the heartbeat in my ears. "Slow, deep breaths, love."

"He is full off shit," I gasp, still hyperventilating. The sound of tearing fabric where my hands still grip the armchair for dear life helps bring me back a little. "Tell me he is full of shit."

"Yes, tell her, Zoltan," Soren chirps a little too happy for his wellbeing.

"I did not know." That strange lilt that sometimes enters Zoltan's voice should calm me as it always does.

It doesn't.

It makes me see red, as a matter a fact.

"I do have a theory on this." Soren keeps talking while I battle the panic attack and the murderous tendencies clawing at me. "Your bloodline accepts all those you have exchanged blood with as part of what is yours. Humans tell tales about dragons hoarding, but that cannot be further from the truth. We simply value what we call ours and guard it viciously. With your history of getting in peculiar situations and always finding yourself at the wrong place at the wrong time, you have exchanged blood with more than just Fenrir."

Soren's voice fades into the background. I can hear him talking, but my mind flashes back to that first day when I came to the Daywalker Academy. When the portal was attacked and I was dazed enough for Zoltan to have to carry me to his rooms. I drank Fenrir's blood that night, which left him unconscious for a long time. After that, I kept pushing Zoltan away until the night he found me on the third floor and let me drink from him. Did he know what was going to happen? I would hate to think that he was manipulative enough to trick me into doing what I wanted. Zoltan is cunning, but he's always honest when it comes down to something like this. Right?

Astara being within an inch from her life floats to my mind next. She was attacked by the hunters and I gave her my blood. Then Daren giving his when the bomb blasted us off the road in Myst's car, along with Leo. Zoltan's face, his lips twisted and a feral expression on his face while inside that cage, and I allowed him to drink me almost to death then. If Myst hadn't pushed him off me and given me her blood, I wouldn't be here. Acid burns the back of my throat as I try to swallow the bile.

Did all of them know what they were doing?

By not asking if I wanted the bonds the blood created, were all of them stealing a piece of my safety? Were they pretending they were doing it for selfless reasons under the pretense of helping?

Am I pathetic enough to see friendships, and dare I say love in places where nothing but survival played a part?

Is anything in my life even real?

"Drake." Zoltan barking my name snaps me out of my wallowing.

"Were you going to tell me?" I don't care how hollow my words sound because my insides are way hollower than my words in this moment.

"It changes nothing." The sincerity in his voice lifts my head so I can look at him.

"For whom? Me or you?"

"As I said, my theory …" Soren butts in.

"I don't give a fuck about you or your theory right now." Snarling at him makes him take a step away from me. "I will deal with you in a moment." There is a lisp to my speech from the fangs throbbing in my gums.

"For either of us, love." For the second time, Zoltan allows me to see him. Really see him without the walls he built to hide himself from the world. His face swims in my vision from the unshed tears filling my eyes. "I knew what you were to me the first time I saw you."

"Not the night I came to the academy."

"No."

"When you saved me from the shadows." Not a question, but he still answers.

"Yes."

"Were you planning on telling me the rest?" As soon as the words are out, I hold my breath, dread drilling a hole inside me. I'm not even sure what the right answer to that is.

"Not until I knew for certain. It is not something you should guess at, at least that is how I feel about it."

I believe him.

As much as I hate to hear it, I know he is telling the truth. Not just by the sincerity on his face but by the truth ringing true through our bond. I want to shrink away from it even while I want to cling to it harder.

I'm a mess.

Leaning back on the armchair, I refuse to let Zoltan's flinch get to me. I may not blame him for everything, but I am still angry that he has kept things from me. My focus turns to Soren, who by some miracle has stayed quiet long enough to get some information out of Zoltan. And to think I couldn't get him talking a week ago. Who knew I'd be praying to all the gods for the Dragon Blood to keep his mouth shut?

"What can I so I don't feel like I'm missing a part of myself because of the broken oath?" Pinning Soren under a glare, I watch him like a hawk. If a muscle twitches wrong I'm going to go straight for his throat, even if it kills me.

"Fully form the bond you freely accepted with Zoltan." The ancient Fae looks like I'm taking his firstborn, all gloomy and butthurt.

"We did that." Like hell I'll tell Soren the details of how many times Zoltan and I have exchanged blood while he had me pinned with his cock inside of me. Judging by the vampire's smoldering gaze, he remembers each of them, too.

"He will have to speak the words, and I will need to

witness." Folding his arms over his chest, Soren pursed his lips. "This might not be a bad thing."

"Are you listening to yourself or do you just let whatever comes to your head pop out of your mouth?" I breathe slowly, refusing to let anger take over my rational thought. Nothing good has come out of it so far.

"I will do it." The hungry, too-blue eyes do not move away from my face, and my stomach clenches in response to Zoltan's deep voice.

"I shall bring my blade." Soren whirls out of the dining hall like the wind.

The dread redoubles in my gut. The Dragon Blood is acting too eager when only ten minutes ago he did nothing but complain about it.

Somehow, I have a feeling Zoltan and I just jumped from the cooking pan into the fire.

Chapter Four

Waiting for Soren to return turns out to be more painful than anything else I've experienced so far. My emotions keep going from excited, to shitless scared, and then back so fast it's making me dizzy. Lost in my own thoughts, I jump off the armchair when someone clears their throat at the entrance of the dining hall. This damn room never has anything good happen in it, not since the day I originally found it.

"Zoltan, you are needed in the training rooms." The shifter shuffles from foot to foot, nervously darting his gaze everywhere else but at us. "There is an argument that will turn bloody if it isn't stopped."

Absentmindedly, I watch the male that I've never seen before, noticing the fine sheen on his upper lip and the beads of sweat gathering around his hairline. The slight tremor of his hands doesn't go unnoticed, either. I file everything in my head while I stare dispassionately at him. There are more pressing matters at the front of my mind.

Zoltan begins standing, but halfway up he stops at an

awkward half crouch as if he has changed his mind. He's probably not sure whether to stay or go. With everything coming at us from all sides, and with the crazy crap Soren no doubt couldn't wait to bring up, I can't blame him. I also won't hold him back. We can't afford to start killing each other here, not when Roberti may very well unleash literal hell on us at any moment. As much as I want to cling to him and as much as I wish he could hide me from the harsh truths I'm facing, I wave him off.

"Just go deal with it." Giving his hand a reassuring squeeze, I don't turn to watch him leave, focusing entirely on Tenebris still stretched across my feet. "I'll be here when you get back."

"I won't be long." His boots beat a steady rhythm on the floors until they fade.

"What in all the worlds is happening, Tenebris?" The shifter lifts his face to mine as I lean over him, tracing my fingers over his smooth fur. "Is it a blessing or a curse?" Cold sweat drenches the back of my shirt just thinking about what Soren said.

Offspring.

My hand, as if it has a mind of its own, reaches for my flat stomach, and Tenebris zeroes in on the movement with laser focus. Catching myself at the last second, I snatch it away and fist my fingers until the nails pierce the skin of my palm. Fury unfurls in my chest, my powers pulsing wildly and making the armchair I'm sitting on rattle. My mouth opens, a string of curses dying on the tip of my tongue when a dull thump echoes from across the room. My head snaps in that direction, and Tenebris bristles at the sound as well.

My gaze jumps from chairs to tables, then I examine the windows and walls, though I find nothing. There is no one there. The yawning emptiness of the large room feels just like the sensation left inside me from the broken oath. The flickering flames create dancing shadows before my eyes, and I watch them in fascination as they shy away from the silvery moonlight that is tracing patterns on the floor through the arched windows. I used to love the night.

Roberti took that away from me first, and now Soren has only added to my hatred for the darkness.

Another dull thump sounds from the far-right side of the hall, but this one is much louder than the last. The place is hidden by thick shadows where neither the flames nor the moonlight can reach it. A slight darkening flickers as if someone or something is moving, and goosebumps erupt over my arms and legs. Tenebris snarls low in his throat, the hairs down his spine prickling.

"Do you see something?" Pushing the question at the panther under my breath without moving my lips, I try to shift on the armchair without being too obvious about it. "I can feel that we are being watched."

And it's true. I can feel the stare like ghostly fingers slithering over me. It makes my skin crawl. With all my senses on high alert, and with a tight grip on Tenebris so he doesn't pounce before we know what we are dealing with, I let my vision shift, releasing the hold I have on my powers. When bright colors dance and twine through the large space, I know my eyes have changed.

I feel her too.

The dragon sharing my body.

We made a tentative truce for the sake of surviving what's yet to come at us since we are both control freaks unwilling to let the other lead. It works for now, but when she pushes her energy through me and it fills my insides to the point of pain while stretching my skin to near bursting, I can't say how long our mutual agreement will last.

The shadow shifts again pulling me back to the present.

The broken and knotted sickly green threads are my first glimpse at what has graced me with its presence. A subtle odor like stale grapes tickles my nostrils, not overpowering but just enough to turn my stomach inside out. Tenebris bristles under my palm, and that's when the creature steps out, revealing itself to me.

"Holy shit you are an ugly motherfucker." The words rush out before I can stop them, and they only make my self-invited guest hiss at me.

Her body is wiry and covered in fine hairs. Even her bare breasts, as tiny as they are, have a dusting on them that make her look more animal than anything else. Large ears stick up on either side of her head just like those of a hyena, while thick, lush curls of hair fall around them reaching past her shoulders. The face is what makes me flinch in disgust.

Large, much too large eyes with bright brown irises watch me unblinkingly, a red pupil expanding and retracting with every breath I take. The skin on her cheeks and forehead is peeling as I watch, leaving the muscle underneath exposed and gleaming in the moonlight. Instead of a nose there are just two holes for her nostrils, while her mouth is only a horizontal slash that reveals two rows of razor sharp teeth when she grins at me.

"What in all the hells are you supposed to be?" I can't stop staring, but mostly it's because I've never seen anything like it.

One second she stares back, the next she pushes off the floor and sails through the air with both arms raised over her head. Claws as long as daggers burst from her fingertips just as she drops down in front of me, slashing in a wide arch at my chest. Tenebris pounces, plowing at her stomach and taking her down hard. They roll for a few feet before she takes hold of the panther and throws him off her like he is a dirty rag. I'm already up and moving before Tenebris lands on all fours, which is an accomplishment for him after flopping like a noodle through the air.

We both circle the creature as she scrambles to her feet.

"I see Roberti is still playing crazy scientist, huh?" My dragon sends waves of excitement through me, and I know she is itching to test her powers against the creature.

She flips around and follows every move I make, hissing like a feral beast. With no indication that she's about to move again, she jumps high over my head and drops right on top of me. At the last second I dance away, letting her hit the floor hard enough to crack it. The stench intensifies and I gag, putting as much distance as I can between us. She is trying to jump me from above and either crack my spine or carve me open with her claws.

Tenebris hits her body from the side and brings her down again. Taking advantage of it, I bounce on the balls of my feet and join the tumble of limbs. Searing pain makes me gasp when she catches me with her swiping claws, ripping the skin on my upper back and shoulder open. Cocking my arm, I punch her right in the center of her face where her nose should be. Black blood sprays across my face, and when I glance at her, it drips down her chin while she grins at me just like before.

"How did you get in here?" My question is followed by multiple punches to her face, the skin on my knuckles ripping open from the impact to her skull.

Placing a hand at the center of my chest, she shoves me off her and sends my body flying through the air. I hear something snap when my back collides with one of the long tables, and the thing breaks into splinters. When the sickly-green knotted threads of her energy brighten before my blurry eyes, I roll to the side in time to avoid another one of her jumps. Fear and rage burn through me, and it takes my breath away. But they aren't *my* feelings. Zoltan knows something is wrong and his emotions are bursting through our bond. The feelings leave me dazed for longer than I can afford. A kick to my head has me rolling further down the room and away from the creature.

"I'm going to rip you apart limb from limb." Groaning, I lift on my hands and knees, breathing through the pain so I can jump on my feet. "That fucking hurt."

Tenebris tries to pounce on her again, his jaws snapping to get a taste of her, but this time she swats him away like a pesky fly. The creature might be ugly as hell, but that doesn't stop her from being incredibly strong. Not something you would guess just by looking at her.

"Die." Bloody saliva bubbles out of her mouth when she hisses the words like a snake.

"I'd rather not, but thanks for the offer."

Knowing that stubbornness won't get me anywhere, and in this case it might get me killed, I let the dragon take over. My body becomes more pliable and flowy as my arms raise and my knees bend into a fighting stance. The creature throws herself at me, but this time I'm ready. Taking hold of one of her arms and placing my other hand on her hip, I lift her over my head and slam her thin body on the ground. The crunching of bones is like music to my ears. I straddle her while she is down, pressing her arms close to her sides with my thighs as I snatch one broken leg from the table. For a second, fear flashes through the light brown of her eyes, but all life dims when the thick wooden leg breaks through her chest and pins her to the floor.

My harsh breathing echoes off the walls through the suddenly-quiet dining hall.

"Francesca." Zoltan's shout precedes him through the entrance.

"I'm fine." Pushing off the creature, I stand just in time for him to snatch me to his chest. "I had a visitor."

"What the hell is that?" The feral growl in his voice tilts my lips up.

"Roberti has too much time on his hands it seems."

Tenebris circles the body and sniffs it, his growl rumbling in his chest like a running motor. I wiggle my fingers to call him to me and away from it. He follows my call begrudgingly, but his eyes stay locked on it.

"Maybe we should pay him a visit?" Craning my neck, I look up at Zoltan's face.

"It might be time, yes." His arms tighten around me.

"I have the dagger," Soren announces from the doorway, but he stops dead in his tracks when he sees the dead creature.

"Your dagger can wait." Ignoring his scowl, I tug Zoltan and Tenebris out of the dining hall, leaving the Dragon Blood to examine my kill.

How's that for making him proud?

Chapter Five

The fact that those who ran when they heard the commotion (and probably saw Zoltan running through the building like his ass was on fire) part before me when I exit the dining hall may have more to do with the vampire looming at my back than me.

Or so I want to believe.

The idea that I've become someone they fear doesn't sit well with me. Even after their symbolic fist to the chest greeting they bestowed on me, I'm not really convinced it's simply a newfound respect for a half blood. Dragon Blood or not, I'll always be lacking in the eyes of the pure bloods.

"Why did Soren call you Blood King?" I finally murmur under my breath when we exit the double doors and step outside.

Zoltan pretends like he is scanning the area, but I see the side-eyed glance he gives me, and I don't miss the slight stiffening of his shoulders. Since everyone that has met him knows he is more stubborn than a mule and has the same level of arrogance as Fenrir, I wait him out. If I keep asking or I push him too hard, he will clam up.

Or lie.

My jaw clenches in frustration.

"Well?" So much for waiting him out. "I would like think we are past the point of you hiding things from me. Right?" I pinch my thigh because that last word sounds like a question, and there really should never be any doubt about this.

"Right."

Oh, great. The one-word wonder has made an appearance. I almost missed him.

The moon is looming over the forest like she is bending over to smell the scent of dew on the leaves and the heavy smell of the damp soil. With the silence surrounding us, the occasional hoot of an owl or the chirp of a cricket is the only thing adding to the crunching noises our boots make on the gravel. And if the silver orb gets any lower, she will look like she's devouring the trees. A warm red and orange glow falls over us from the large windows of the building to our left, making our shadows extend and dance as if they have a mind of their own. In my peripheral vision I catch the bright eyes of shifters pop in and out through the trunks of the trees, the guards ever watchful of anything that dares move around here. Too bad they didn't pay attention when the creature decided to pay me a visit.

"Where are we going?" Zoltan's soft, deep voice has butterflies swarming in my lower belly.

"Now you are asking?" Ignoring his smirk and raised eyebrow, I glare in front of me at an invisible foe. "That should've been the first thing out of your mouth before you followed me."

"You didn't give me an option to ask, or decline for that matter."

"If I tell you to jump off the building and land on your head, would you do it?" My half-cocky grin is frozen on my lips when he shrugs.

"If you push me off it I'll have no other option but to do what you want."

"Poor Zoltan. He has no say in his life. The mighty Daywalker is being bullied by a female." I'm not sure why I'm getting so angry with him. Well aware that I'm pushing him so I can start a fight, I'm still not able to stop the words from coming out of my mouth.

Stopping in his tracks, he snatches my upper arm and tugs at me until I face him. The breath is lodged in my throat, and it's as thick as a fist, which prevents me from swallowing. His eyes are glowing like stars on his face, and the two sharp points of his fangs are poking out from under his upper lip, denting the bottom one. His features sharpen before my eyes. And then his fists clench, his nostrils flaring and the muscles of his chest and arms are bulging.

Everything I am reacts to the aggression wafting off him in waves. The dragon blood warms my veins, my powers stretching as if in answer. My skin feels too tight to contain me. My body follows through by getting more pliable, my legs shifting so I stand on the balls of my feet with my knees slightly bent as if ready to attack. Bright colors burst to life all around me, my eyes changing to that of a dragon at the same time as my gums throb from the extending of my fangs.

"You are bleeding." Words garbled around the fangs that are as thick and as long as my pinky, Zoltan looks me up and down with such an intense stare I involuntarily shiver.

A jolt goes through me when he reaches for me. The ground under our feet trembles in reaction, making the wolves in the forest sing a warning song. The howls get closer so fast I can feel the heat of the pack at my back. Low snarls are accompanied by the feral cry of a couple of felines, too. All of them are at my back facing Zoltan, my magic and connection to this place forcing them to protect me at any cost.

A nagging at the back of my mind tries to pull my attention away, but I'm too far gone at the moment to do anything about it. Alarms blare in my head that this is not normal, but yet again I'm a passenger in my own body. Zoltan stops with his hand raised between us, his eyes narrowed to slits at the shifters behind me. A couple of them whimper when his power slams at us as hard as a slap, but not one of them backs down.

"Ms. Drake." Snapping at me, his upper lip curls in a snarl. "You are bleeding. I need to see the wound." He hasn't used that "Ms. Drake" bullshit for a while, so it's enough to jolt me out of whatever is clouding my head.

"What the fuck is going on?" Pushing the words though clenched teeth, my whole body is racked by tremors, though I still can't relax from my fighting stance. "Don't." My shout is enough to prevent him from moving when I see that he is about to reach for me again. "I can't control my reaction right now, and I will attack you."

With a slanted gaze he assesses me again, and then his hand drops to his side. I almost cry from the relief that I won't have to hurt him. Zoltan is the strongest male I know, but when the creature inside me gets defensive like it is now I have no doubt in my mind that he will get hurt. He will give me a run for my money, but he will lose at the end. It will kill me inside if I bring such a magnificent beast to his end. Having the guards still at my back will only serve as a distraction, nothing else.

Closing his eyes, Zoltan's chin drops to his chest and his shoulders hunch inward as if he's been punched. I suck in a harsh breath that makes the shifters snarl and hiss. The spike of fear is replaced by dread when I watch his body grow before my eyes. The thick horns twist and curl around his head to form a horrifying crown as his muscles double, twitching from the strain of his tight fists. My head tilts up until a kink develops in my neck, but at least I can see his face. I should be paying closer attention to the wicked claws protruding from his fingers, but instead I'm frozen in awe at the sight of him in his true form. Not that it will help him much.

Those extraordinary eyes fixate on my face with such intensity my knees buckle.

"I said, 'you are bleeding.'" The foreign lilt to his words turns my insides to mush.

The creature inside me perks and purrs, my chest vibrating from it.

"Dè a tha thu a 'dol a dhèanamh mu dheidhinn?" Sultry words spill out of my mouth, my voice unrecognizable when I ask him what he is planning to do about it.

He attacks.

I have never been hit by a truck—which is something that will come out straight from the mouths of humans— but I'm pretty sure this is how it must feel. The air whooshes out of my lungs when his fist slams in my chest. My body flies in the air, my limbs flailing until I hit the trunk of a tree a few yards away. Bones crunch when my spine clashes against the harsh bark, and I drop on my hands and knees panting and gasping. Silence thick enough to be cut with a blade falls over the place, the anticipation of the magic so palpable I think I can reach a hand out and touch it. A soft chuckle pierces the air.

It's coming from me.

As the laughter grows in volume, my head lifts and I watch confusion bloom over Zoltan's face. My back burns where the broken bones knit together, healing a lot faster than ever before. With that comes the memory of the creature raking its claws over me before I killed it, ripping the skin on my shoulder and back. It pulses, but I can tell it's not closing. It must be what Zoltan was talking about. I have blood all over me from killing the damn thing, and it stunk pretty bad when it was alive. Coming outside must've cleared away that putrid stench so he could finally smell my own blood again, though it still doesn't explain why he attacked me.

Tendrils of my hair escape my braid and hang in front of my eyes when I grin at him. Swiping the back of my hand over my mouth, I wipe away the blood that is trickling from my lips before my tongue darts out to lick the remainder off. I keep steady eye contact with Zoltan the entire time, my grin stretching wider when his nostrils flare.

"Is dòcha gu bheil thu nad leannan airidh air às deidh a h-uile càil, vampire." My chuckle pebbles the skin on my arms. *"You might be a deserving lover after all, vampire,"* I told him. Whatever game the Dragon Blood in me is playing, I don't like it.

I start fighting to regain control of my body.

Pushing off the ground, I crack my neck and roll my shoulders to remove the stiffness from the impact with the now-tilted tree. I guess it was uprooted when I slammed into it. Go figure. Roots as thick as my thighs poke up from the upturned earth at my feet. Peeking at Zoltan through my lashes, there is nothing I can do to wipe off the small smile curling the corners of my lips.

"Where were you going, Francesca?" Let it never be said that Zoltan will give up a fight. The jerk is still adamant that I answer his question.

"I …" my voice trails off, both eyebrows lowering and tightening my forehead. "I …" I have no idea where I was going. There is no way I'm going to tell him that, but the realization is enough to give me some of my control back.

"Let us go inside." One of his wicked hands with those sharp claws is trying to beguile me to go to him.

"No." Hissing angrily at him, my fists ball at my sides.

"I will not let you go anywhere when you are not your-self. Did that creature use a poisoned blade?" He moves parallel with me when I start inching to the side, his eyes locked on every move I make.

"No." At least I have that much of my rational brain left to tell him the truth. "It raked me with its claws."

"You will come with me inside, Francesca." His stub-born look is replaced by determination.

"Carson nach toir thu orm?" I'm saying one thing in that damn tongue twister language I'll never be able to pronounce if not for the creature inside me, while in my head I'm screaming the total opposite: *"No, don't take me. Don't you dare take me anywhere."*

Zoltan throws his head back and laughs.

"Mar a mhiannacheadh tu." All the oxygen leaves my lungs for a different reason when he whispers the words telling me, *as you wish*, and a sinful smile dances on his lips.

That's all the warning I get.

One second we are in a standoff with a few yards sepa-rating us from each other, and the next he is in front of me, his huge hand taking a hold of my shoulder. Moving on pure instinct alone, I twirl around, spinning under his arm and getting a good grip on his forearm. Taking a running step, I flip my legs across his torso, releasing his arm and using his body as a surfboard to glide over until I twist to his side and land on my feet behind him. Lifting my leg, I kick the center of his lower back, sending him crashing and sprawling over the poor uprooted tree.

He doesn't stay down long at all. I have no time to gloat before he is in my face again, his fists and claws coming from all sides and looking for an opening to score a hit. My own arms and legs are moving just as fast to block each punch and kick, my shins screaming in protest each time one of his boots connects to them. Our harsh breathing is the only thing I can hear, the fast breaths sawing in and out of our lungs. I can't help but wonder why the stupid guards don't attack or at least make a sound. Now is the perfect time for a distraction, and I'm starting to regret the cocky attitude I had earlier when I thought Zoltan had a chance of losing this fight. The adrenaline coursing through me clears out my mind and I finally identify the urge that made me come out here.

"I need to get to the portal," I tell Zoltan, each word strained coming out in a huff.

"Why?" The question is a snarl, which pisses me off.

"How the fuck should I know, asshole." Dancing away from a particular swipe that would've carved my stomach open, I glare at him. "Cut me open, why don't ya?"

My talking earns me a smirk and a kick to the gut that sends me on my back sliding over the gravel, which is scratching the shit out of my exposed skin. I'm never wearing a tank top around Zoltan again. Bringing my knees to my chest, I kick out and jump to my feet, but that only gives me a second to see the massive fist coming for my face.

I think I hear Zoltan mumble something like "forgive me my love," but pain explodes in my head as gravity shoves me to the ground and I'm sure I imagined it. It's the second time in less than ten seconds that my back hits the ground, and my eyes cross as blood gushes down my chin. The scariest thing I see before I pass out is Soren standing at the window on the second floor watching us.

Does he know what's going on with me? Even if he doesn't, why doesn't he come stop us? Furthermore, does he have something to do with it? A million questions flash through my mind in less time than it takes me to blink.

And then I pass out.

Chapter Six

The angry voices cut off when a pained groan rips from my lips. I try my best to turn to my side, but my stomach churns so bad I have to grind my teeth so I don't lose the contents all over myself or whoever is standing so close to me. Zoltan, no doubt. The jerk deserves it, but I'm well aware that I would've done something very stupid if he didn't stop me.

Soren's distorted face through the glass of the window floats behind my closed eyelids. Did I really see him, or was he a hallucination from whatever drug the creature had on its claws? Just thinking about it sends excruciating pain through my skull, which elicits another groan from me.

"Francesca?" Zoltan murmurs a second before his hand cups my cheek and he turns my face to him.

"There are other ways to knock me out apart from punching me in the face. You know that, right?" Not that I blame him, but it tickles me to see him squirm. It's impossible not to feel the spike of adrenaline coming off of him. "You should've been a shifter for as many times as you find yourself in the dog house." Nothing could stop the curl of my lips when he snatches his hand back.

"I told him he'll regret it when you wake up." Astara's voice is full of amusement, and it forces my eyes open.

Blinking away my blurry vision, I turn my head and look around. I'm not surprised to find myself in Zoltan's rooms. The jerk is territorial. What does surprise me is seeing Leo leaning a shoulder on the wall and watching me with an exhausted look on his usually grinning face. His green eyes stay on mine, but he doesn't say a word. I look away, finding Astara standing next to her brother, her hand fisted in his t-shirt and bunching it on his chest as if she is preventing him from running away. It would've been funny, and I'm about to say a bunch of things that come to my mind that will give him a hard time, but her appearance stops me from uttering any of it.

Her once glossy hair is dull and sticking out in frizzy strands from the messy bun she attempted on top of her head. The flawless skin I was jealous of looks etiolated, her cheeks sunken and making the dark circles under her eyes stand out like smudges on her face. Over her shoulder I see Daren warily watching me from further in the room, his hair sticking out in all directions like he's been running his fingers through it and tugging on it. I haven't seen the two of them since they took over their places in the Order, and I stupidly believed they were ignoring me. Come to think of it, the couple of times I saw Leo it was brief, too, and he was lacking the typical jokes and arrogance he usually sports.

"What's going on with the three of you?" Blurting out the first thing that comes to mind, I cringe as I push off the bed and swing my legs over the side.

"You should see yourself before you talk." Astara

attempts a joke, causing Zoltan to grumble something under his breath.

"It takes him"—Hitching a thumb in her brother's direction, I grin at her—"knocking me out to see you. Bloody nose or not, I'll take it."

A paw-sized hand prevents me from standing up. Zoltan grips my shoulder and pushes me down on the bed as I glare at him, but I say nothing when I catch the determined jut of his chin. Astara shoulders him away so she can to sit next to me.

"Seriously, Franky. How do you feel?" The worry on my friend's face makes me sigh.

"As good as you look." It comes out in a huff as I wiggle further to the center of the bed to make room for her.

"Be nice." She pokes her long nail into my thigh.

"You are my friend because I'm not nice." That broadens her smile, which also brings a little of the sparkle back in her eyes. "There is nothing wrong with me now. No need to stay in bed. I feel fine."

"Drake, did a portal open before the creature attacked you?" I turn to look at Leo when he speaks, recoiling into the pillows the same second because Tenebris's huge head pops up in front of me. I didn't see him stretched out next to the bed when I attempted to get up.

"If there was one, I didn't feel it, and I definitely didn't see it." Frowning, I reach for the panther's head to scratch his ears when he leans his chin on the bed, his gaze intently focused on my face. "There was a shift in the energy … Tenebris sensed it at the same time as me. I'm not exactly sure what got my attention and made me look for something before she showed herself. I can't really remember now. What?" The question comes out harsher than I intended it when they all glance at each other.

"No disturbance was recorded, so that tells me no magic was involved to open a gate for the creature." Daren sounds as tired as he looks.

"You mean she was here longer and just decided to show herself?" Unable to stay where I am, I lift up, curling the knees to my chest and wrapping my arms around them. My mind is spinning with what that creature could've been doing left alone in the academy. "But how? Someone would've known if she passed our portals, no? Even if a mole helped her hide, they had to get her through it first."

"Agreed." Since Daren doesn't sound very confident, I keep my gaze steadily on him until he squirms.

"Right?" My second attempt at asking for confirmation just adds to the tension in the room.

"We could've missed it." Astara gives the mage a side-eyed glance, and my stomach clenches when I see how uncomfortable she is about pointing that out.

"Now is the right time for everyone to stop dodging bullets and speak plainly. If she managed to slip your notice, there could be others too. That thing was not easy to kill. Think of the damage something like that could do to the others we have here." Scrubbing a hand over my face, I puff up my cheeks before blowing out a long breath out. "Imagine if they can get out of the gates and roam through Sienna. It's a bad idea to keep secrets."

"We are not keeping secrets." The hurt plastered all over Daren's face has more to do with him hiding shit from me since I've known him than from my accusation right now. His fingers stab through his thick hair and he tugs on it in frustration, which makes it look like a horn on one side of his head. "Things are not as easy as we anticipated when we took over as members of the Order."

That gains him stern, angry looks from Leo and Astara.

"Not easy in what way?" My gaze darting from one face to the next, I try my best not to scream at them. It's like pulling teeth with my bare hands to get any answers from this bunch of stubborn mules. "It's not hurting you in any way, is it?" Panic ripples through me at that. "Is it?"

"Not the way you think." Astara is fast to assure me, taking my hand in hers. "It's overwhelming, and we still can't control it."

"It's draining their lives." Zoltan speaks for the first time since calling my name to wake me. "Do not lie to her." Folding his thick arms across his chest, he looks down his nose at his sister.

"Soren knew this?" When Astara winces, I have to consciously uncurl my fingers since they are tightened around her hand. "He was the one encouraging you to take their place. If he knew this was going to happen, what was his motivation? It couldn't be just because he thought they were compromised by Roberti. He even helped. So why would he be looking away now? To what end?"

"Franky, calm down." I realize I'm shaking in rage, my upper lip curling over extended fangs, and when Astara gingerly reaches for me, she drops her hand before making contact.

"We are searching the entire area, including inside each of the rooms." Leo pushes off the wall and starts pacing. "We haven't found anyone else."

"Yet." Pointing that out earns me a scowl from Zoltan.

"If there are more, we will know within the hour." The confidence I hear in his deep voice calms me a little. Not enough to ignore the reason why I'm so angry.

"Did you find out what kind of a poison she used on me?" I forcibly keep my body still while shivers claw at my back.

"I'm not sure it was a poison." Daren looks down at his hands, a line forming between his brows and puckering his forehead. "I can't be certain, but I believe it was a secretion uniquely to her, whatever mixed species she was. To know more I'll have to check the body. I wanted to see that you were well before I go there."

"I tasted your blood." Zoltan narrows his eyes on me, daring me to say something about it. "There was no trace of anything in it, yet the effects were strong. Even unconscious, I had to restrain you so you didn't go to the portal."

"Where is Soren now?" When he cocks an eyebrow thinking I'm ignoring his comment, I wave him off. "I thought I was hallucinating before I passed out, but something doesn't sit well with me here."

"Hallucinating about what?" A muscle jumps in his jaw and his gaze is so slanted it looks like he is squeezing his eyes shut.

"That he was watching the two of us from the window on the second floor."

"He was acting very curious about the creature. He said he wants to look at the body. When they were taking it to the infirmary, he left with them," Daren answers my original question.

My mouth opens, but I lose my train of thought when Daren jerks his spine straight, his head snapping in the direction of the window overlooking the forest outside. His fingers twitch and sparks like tiny firecrackers burst from them. Astara jumps to her feet, and I scramble off the bed to join her.

"Someone is trying to open the portal forcibly." Daren sounds distracted as he stands frozen in place.

"Trying how?" Dropping on my knees, I search for my

boots, but I don't see them anywhere in the room. "They are opening it now?"

"No." Sounding confused, Astara walks up to Daren and places her hand on his forearm. "It feels like they are testing it. Not opening it, at least not yet."

Popping my head up from under the bed, I almost head-butt Tenebris, who was crawling under it as if we are playing a game. "Testing from the other side, correct?"

"It's hard to tell." When I turn to Leo, he is frowning, his wolf coming to the surface to look through his eyes.

Dread washes over me and my lips numb, tingling like crazy.

"Zoltan." I have no idea how my voice sounds because I'm unable to hear it thanks to the thundering of my heart in my ears, but his head turns in my direction so fast I'm not sure how his neck doesn't break. "The book."

He stiffens, anger and confusion warring on his face long enough to bring me out from the brink of passing out. The dark spots dancing on the edges of my vision clear out, and using Tenebris as a clutch, I jump to my feet.

"There is no time to hide stupid shit. We trust them, plus none of them will want to brave your alien thingy with those tentacles of death. Not unless they wanted to steal it. Check the book."

Zoltan moves to obey without grumbling about it for a change, and I lean on Tenebris further, the shifter angling his body closer to better support my weight. It's either the fear that the book might be stolen, or whatever the creature did to me that is still making me unsteady on my feet. Bitterness coats my tongue as I watch unblinking, my chest burning from the breath I'm holding. I know we are screwed the second he removes the tile on the roof. No tentacles reach out like in a horror movie, the gaping black hole mocking us with its emptiness.

Zoltan's hand lowers slowly to the side, but he still has his face tilted up as if he can't believe what he is looking at. The silence in the room is choking me, pressing on my shoulders with such force I'm surprised I'm not pushed into the floor waist deep. Painfully slow, Zoltan turns, his eyes burning into mine over his shoulder. Three attempts at talking fail before I manage to push the words through my numb lips.

"It was a distraction."

Daren is out the door so fast a light breeze ruffles my hair. My feet are moving on their own, and before I know it, I'm right on his heels, everyone else following right behind me.

Chapter Seven

"Francesca." Zoltan is breathing down my neck even while we run.

"I need to see where Soren is." Veering off to the left, I bolt across the open foyer of the academy heading straight for the infirmary. Leo, Daren, and Astara disappear through the front doors. "You should go help them out. I know squat about how to stop someone who's trying to open a portal."

"No." That's all from the jerk. Just no.

The vice tightening my chest squeezes so hard my breath comes in short gasps, but I don't stop. Arguing with him will be pointless. The vampire became clingier after I accepted our bond, apparently taking it as an agreement to be attached at the hip. As if just by saying the words I created this invisible cord tying us together, and the leash is incredibly short. If you see me, he will be a couple of feet away at best. He must've learned that trick from Tenebris. The panther is loping down the hallways and stairs at the same speed as me, his body constantly brushing against my hand or thigh. I'm moving up in life with not one, but two pains in my ass now.

When I reach the double doors of the infirmary, I burst through them and nearly collide with the nurse Aspen. Her eyes widen for a split second before she plants herself in my way, bracing as if she is about to fight me to prevent me from going any further inside. Her red hair is up in a bun with pencils sticking out of it every which way, and her lips are pressed in a thin white line while she glares at me. The dark gray scrubs she is wearing tighten around her thighs and shoulders when she slightly bends her knees. Crazy female.

"Soren," I snap, trying to shoulder my way pass her. "Where is he?"

Snatching my arm, she yanks me back and almost mushes me against Zoltan's chest. "No one gets in that room until I'm done."

"Is he in there?" Grinding my teeth, I remind myself that fighting with her will take more time.

"Soren went through the sanitizing chamber and changed clothing before entering. You two will not go in there." Tightening her grip on me, Aspen holds me at arm's length with a stubborn tilt to her chin.

"*I* killed the thing; my germs are already all over it." Dismissing her, I jerk on my arm, but she clings to it for dear life. "You can hold Zoltan hostage if you like. He definitely should stay outside."

"Both of you will not go anywhere near it. Here my word is law." I'm too late to see her other hand moving until the needle is almost piercing my shoulder.

At the last moment I twist, bending my body like a contortionist and slapping the syringe to the side. The thick long needle sinks into Zoltan's shoulder, and he takes a step back a moment too late. His back hits the doors that bounced closed after our entrance, and he blinks at me very slowly before dropping his chin to look at what's sticking out of his body.

Tenebris snarls even as he slinks away from him, his ears pinned to the side of his head.

"Oh, shit," Aspen breathes, dropping the hand she was still holding mine with.

"It's not bad." A hysterical giggle escapes me. "Not like you injected him, right?" When I don't get an answer, I glance at her. Her red hair is standing out stark against her blanched face. "You did. What was in that thing?"

"Tranquilizer." Her lips barely move.

Zoltan jerks his head up, his murderous gaze locking on Aspen with so much malice that even I take a step back with her. Her hand latches onto my forearm for a totally different reason this time.

"How much tranquilizer?" We both move a step back when Zoltan stumbles toward us.

"To knock down a house." The quiver in her voice does not help my anxiety.

"You were going to stab me with it?" We take another step back because Zoltan moves toward us again. I'm just not sure how long we can keep this crazy dance up.

"It's not personal." Sounding defensive, Aspen digs her nails into my skin. "Do you know how thick headed the males in this building are? When I knock them out, I need them not to get up again, at least until I have a chance to tie them to one of the beds."

"If the situation was different, I might tell you that sounds kinky." My snickering is hoarse and strained.

Tenebris circles Zoltan almost as if he has found weakness in his prey.

"Tenebris, don't you dare." Hissing at the shifter, I keep Zoltan in my sight in case he decides to pounce. "Get your furry ass away from him."

"He is going to be so pissed." The laugh coming from Aspen is more of a hiccupped sob.

"You'll be fine." Not even I believe my own words when Zoltan snarls. "I do shit like this to him all the time."

"You tranquilize him?" Forgetting all about the furious vampire, her head jerks in my direction.

"What? No." Zoltan lurches at us, and I yank her away to the side. "But I have stabbed him, broken quite a few of his bones, cracked my knee on his jewels, fought him many times, and I'm pretty sure I piss him off enough that he thinks about killing me at least a few times a day. As I said, you'll be fine."

"Oh, dear fates … I'm going to die."

"Didn't you hear what I said?" I check to make sure she didn't stab herself with the needle as well. She's not making sense.

"You are his mate." Aspen looks at me pointedly before ducking under Zoltan's flying fist. Good thing he is slow or he would've cracked her skull for sure. "I am not." Panting, she scurries to the other side of the waiting room.

Telling her when he is furious it doesn't matter who you are goes unsaid when Zoltan stops moving, swaying twice on his feet before his eyes close and he drops like a chopped-down tree. The hard thump when his body hits the floor makes Aspen and I jump a foot off the ground before we look at each other. Her green eyes look too big on her face, probably the same way as mine.

"How do we tie him up?" Aspen almost swallows her tongue at my question. "Do you want to die?"

That propels her into motion, and between us we drag

him to one of the rooms with a bed bolted to the floor. I'm not sure what kind of procedures they do in these types of rooms and I'm not going to ask. She is working meticulously as if she's done this way too many times before. I remember Fenrir and Leo freaking out and acting like scared children around her. Now I understand why. I'll be keeping one eye open from now on when it comes to Aspen.

"What?" she mumbles when she sees me watching her.

"I'm kinda in an awe to be honest." Snorting at her frown, I wave a hand over Zoltan's body. "Quite impressive if I may say so."

"All of them are stubborn and think they are invincible or smarter than a female." Tugging on the metal cuffs around Zoltan's wrists to make sure they are secure, her face twists in a grimace. "After being yelled at, kicked when I try to help them because they are like spoiled younglings, and being looked down upon, I had to make a choice. I will either teach them a lesson, or stop doing what I love to do." Squaring her shoulders, she gives me an even look, bracing for my reaction, I guess. "I will not be looked down upon."

"I can respect that." Giving her a small smile, I glance down at Zoltan. "I also owe you one for this." She doesn't look convinced, but I've wasted enough time. "I must see Soren. Someone is trying to tamper with the portal." Not seeing any harm in telling her that much, I'm already moving out of the room.

"You think it's Roberti?" Rushing past me, she hurries across the waiting room and waves at me to follow her. "You should've said so to begin with."

"I don't make it habit to explain myself or what I'm doing."

The soft creme walls break the sterile look of the infirmary, softening the harsh glint of the stainless steel cabinets and machines that are pushed in the corners. Gray chairs with pale pink cushions must be Aspen's touch judging from the pink fabric attached to the pockets of her gray scrubs. Her head bobs up and down as she leads me to a door almost at the end of the hallway, passing dozens of others which are closed.

"There are many people here at the moment?" Curiosity gets the better of me.

"A few.' Looking over her shoulder, she gives me an eye roll. "Mages and shifters are the worst. The former can't help but show how tough they are by flinging magic around, which usually backfires in some way or another. The latter can't help but be bullies and fight to show their dominance. Like younglings, I'm telling you."

I hear the sounds before we reach the last door on our right. Aspen falters in her steps, then she almost trips so I reach out to grab her in case she goes down. I shouldn't have worried. Nimble as a cat, she skips and bounces a couple of times with both arms outstretched for balance until she is steady enough to dart for the room. I'm right behind her when she pushes the door open, and we spring off each other when she stops abruptly.

"What the actual fuck, Soren." My incredulous shout makes the damn Fae look at me with a huge grin plastered on his face.

"Isn't it marvelous?" Twirling like a ballerina, he misses the claws aiming for his head.

"How is that thing still alive?" Shoving Aspen away, I rush inside to help him.

I regret gloating about how Zoltan is chained to a bed and sleeping right now. Fighting the damn creature once was more than enough for me. Luckily Tenebris doesn't leave me alone, so he slinks around the creature in a way that we have it cornered from all sides between the three of us. My feet slow when I notice the jerky movements of the creature, so unlike how it used to glide the first time I saw her.

"What's wrong with it apart from it not staying dead?" I kick her in the back of her leg to force her to her knees when she tries to pounce on Soren again.

"I gave her some of my blood to see if I can get any information." Soren sounds dismissive and is totally oblivious to my jaw unhinging in shock. "She was awake and moving within half an hour. Do you see, Francesca? This is brilliant news. Whatever Roberti is trying to achieve, it's failing because he is not using Dragon Blood in whatever mutations he is creating. Good thing too that he hasn't realized that yet, I would think." Like a child receiving a new toy they wished to have for a long time, his eyes are sparkling from excitement. "We can study it and get ahead of him."

"I'm going to kill you myself." Grinding my teeth at his pouty face, I kick at the creature again to keep it down when it struggles to get on its feet. "You really are insane."

"How is this possible?" Aspen gasps from the door, finally coming out of her stupor.

"I have my ways." Sniffing arrogantly, Soren crouches on his haunches and peers at the creature as if it's a bug. His hand glides over his platinum hair to push it out of his face and over his still-bare shoulder. Aspen sighs wistfully.

I glare at him.

He pretends not to notice but his lips twitch at the corners.

Ass.

"First of all, she can't speak so your excuse for this clusterfuck doesn't hold. But you know that already." Jabbing

Aspen with my elbow to snap her out of it, I circle next to the Dragon Blood. "You just wanted to cause trouble. Second of all, where is your damn shirt?"

"I do not need it." Tilting his face to look at me, he smirks as if he's enjoying my anger a little too much. "Does it bother you, young dragon?"

"No." Great, I'm sounding like Zoltan now. The poor vampire might have a point about me being insufferable. Especially if I'm acting like Soren.

"It is settled then."

"What?" Confused, I frown at him.

"That I do not need a covering." His chuckle grates on my nerves.

"What are we going to do with it now that you turned it into a zombie?" Choosing not to take his bait, I turn the conversation to more important matters.

"It will not stay alive long."

Pulling his attention back to the creature, I see the calculating gaze flickering over the struggling female on the floor. Guilt at seeing her like this pushes to the front of my mind but I shove it back. She tried to kill me not long ago. There is no mercy when it comes between my life and hers. Not for the first time, I regret not listening to Zoltan when he told me not to wake Soren up. That day when the Order members organized a party for my arrival at the Daywalkers Academy feels like it happened in another life-time. So much shit has happened since then that I can barely remember all the details. With a sigh, I nudge Soren with my foot.

"How long is not long?"

"I do not know." A line forms between his perfectly-shaped eyebrows, and the tip of one pointed ear pokes between his silky hair when he cocks his head to the side.

"The creature was a distraction." I watch him like a hawk for any indication that he knew that. His golden gaze flicks to mine, but it's unreadable. "Someone is poking at the portal as we speak and …" A quick glance tells me Aspen is paying more attention than Soren at the moment, but I throw caution to the wind. "The book was stolen."

Soren jumps up, and I flinch like an idiot. Tenebris, who was as still as a statue until now, hisses at him from the side, but Soren is already moving past me and heading for the door.

"I believe the mage was testing his control," the Fae muses under his breath.

"The mage has a name." After a few steps I stop because I don't know what to do. My gaze goes from Soren's back to the creature on the floor.

"I got this," Aspen says, shooing me away and pulling out another of those tranquilizers from her pocket.

"How many of those do you have on you?" Staring at her pockets doesn't give me x-ray vision, but that doesn't stop me from trying to check for myself.

"Enough." Pressing her lips in a firm line again, she approaches the creature carefully. "Don't try anything, Drake. I like you, but I'll use it on you, too, and I won't bat an eye when I do." An angry roar rattles the walls of the building, and Aspen almost jumps out of her skin. "Oh, no."

"Zoltan is awake." I grin from ear to ear. "You'll jab me with your needles, but only if you don't die today."

"You keep him away from me, and I'll save my needles for the males." She can't fake the bravado she is going for, but I still nod anyway.

"Deal." Turning away, I head for the door with Tenebris at my side. "Just keep that thing out of commission until it's dead for good." Another roar, much louder, echoes through the hallway.

"Is that Zoltan?" Soren's voice floats to my ears and I wink at Aspen over my shoulder.

"I'm not sure, but let's go check." Calling out my reply, I rush after the Fae, but I have to force my lips not to curl up.

I'm going to send Soren to face the pissed off Daywalker, and I'll be watching the bloodbath from the sidelines.

Chapter Eight

To my great disappointment, neither Soren nor Zoltan were smacked around. They are both ruffed up with stoic faces and glaring at each other, but no one is bleeding. I was hoping a fight between them would slap some sense into their stubborn heads. No such luck. Stroking my fingers over Tenebris's head, I watch them both from the corner of my eye, but I keep my mouth shut. At this point, I can handle Soren. It's Zoltan who is itching for me to say something so he can scoop me up and lock me away in a room claiming it's for my own good.

I can feel it.

My forehead scrunches when we enter the open foyer and see everyone rushing around not paying us any attention. They all move with purpose, their spines straight and shoulders stiff. The glow of the flickering flames adds an additional weight to the apprehension turning the otherwise light air as thick as a fog.

Zoltan storms through them, pushing those that are too distracted to notice him aside like he's swatting flies. Soren does the same, looking less like a brute, though he's still just as entitled as always. My skin pebbled with goosebumps, I follow behind them while tugging Tenebris so close to me his side is plastered to my thigh. Dread gnaws at my insides, guilt making me sick because I took too long with Aspen. I enjoy messing with Zoltan, and somehow, my friends always pay the price. The annoyance at the two males for being arrogant evaporates when that thought is rooted to the center of my mind. My feet move faster, my heart jackhammering against my ribs.

"They are all well." Soren turns his head to look at me over his shoulder.

Damn supernatural hearing.

Sucking in deep breaths, I force my heartbeat to slow because I don't want the next comment to come from the vampire, who is fisting his hands with enough force his muscles are twitching all the way up his arms. As furious as he is, Zoltan is mindful enough not to blast me with his power. I feel it stinging my skin like the pincers of million fire ants, but it's bearable. The blast of fresh air and the cool breeze welcome me when we walk out the large front doors, our feet pounding down the few concrete steps to the front yard. What we missed while inside and surrounded by so many bodies we feel immediately.

Magic that makes the trees sway whips through the air, the branches flipping around like waving flags. It smells like ozone when I inhale a sharp breath, and my eyes water when it sears my nostrils. I had every intention of letting the males lead the way, but this propels me forward fast enough that I bump my shoulders off them as I push them apart and bolt around the building. Tenebris keeps pace with me, his body stretching gracefully with each silent loop he makes. Zoltan spits some choice words before his pounding footsteps tell me he is running after me. Without turning around, I know Soren is next to him, as well. When I turn the corner and get a clear view of the open area and the portal, I skid to a stop, the blood curdling in my veins.

"Right there." Zoltan stabs a finger to point to the left side of the portal.

Colors are swirling and flashing, brightening the entire area so much I have to blink a few times to clear my vision. Daren is standing in front of the portal with both arms raised and magic pouring out of his palms so strong it almost looks like long, thick scarves coming out of his hands. Astara and Leo stand on either side of him, each gripping one shoulder to lend him strength. All three of them are swaying slightly, and Daren's lips are moving but no sound reaches my ears. Movement to the left corner of the portal catches my eye and I am finally able to see what Zoltan was pointing at. Three wolves, our guards, are inching closer, looking for an opening in the pulsing and ballooning portal to get to a figure stuck neither in this realm nor the human one. My heart skips a beat when the figure wiggles and I get a glimpse of the book they are holding.

"Not this again." Groaning, I roll my shoulders to alleviate the tension in my muscles.

One of the wolves pounces, his body sailing through the air. I hold my breath and stare unblinkingly until a twisting tendril of magic snaps in his direction, smacking him on the side. Tail over head, the wolf flips through the air until it hits one of the trunks in the tree line, dropping on the ground and not getting up again. A lump in my throat chokes me when another wolf, this one with a pure white coat, passes by his fallen friend before rushing forward to take his place.

"Roberti needs to die, like today." Snarling, I clench my fists hard enough for the nails to pierce the skin of my palms.

"I will help them keep the portal steady." Soren saunters across the grass without a care in the world.

"Which one do you want, the book or whoever stole it?" My words are barely above a whisper, but I know Zoltan hears me.

Strong winds pick up and lash at us from all sides. I watch Soren's bare back, each lean muscle outlined when his hair is picked up in the air. It twists and flips on the wind like silk, and it makes this whole situation unreal. He looks like he is walking under water, each movement graceful as a rainbow of colors dance around him.

"We go together," Zoltan growls, the finality in his voice leaving no room for arguments.

"Obviously. I just need to know which one you want so I can focus on one thing." Annoyed with him, I sigh heavily. "They are stuck, as you can see. Whoever is helping Roberti with the portal is trying to get them out. That's what Daren is trying to prevent, I think. I don't want to waste time arguing with you."

"I'll take the thief, you get the book."

It costs him to agree with me. I know it does, but I give him a smile in thanks. We are both in unfamiliar waters with this whole bond thing, and instead of trying to figure it out together, we pull in opposite directions. I'm more to blame than he is, but I'll never admit it. Not even if my life depends on it. At least he is willing to compromise at the moment.

"I have Tenebris with me, so just focus on the asshole." Pointing out the obvious as I dart around the bigger area with the strongest wind, I call on my magic. "I won't get hurt." On purpose, is the part I say in my head.

He grunts.

We near the place where the wolves are still moving back and forth while trying to go past the lashing magic. It gives me a better view of my friends, and I almost fall flat on my face when I trip. Astara and Leo are not lending Daren strength by placing a hand on his shoulders, they are holding him up. The mage has a slack look on his face, his eyes pure white and staring straight. Fear pierces my chest seeing his sunken cheeks and blanched skin. Despite that, magic keeps pouring out of his hands without pause. My panicked eyes dart around in search of Soren, only finding him when he steps next to Daren.

"Dear Fates. Zoltan, Daren will die if he has to keep this up much longer." Reaching blindly for him, I sag when he takes my hand and tugs me to his chest. "What can I do? I need to help him. I don't know how to help him."

I know I'm blabbering and not making sense, but my rational brain abandoned me when I saw my friend fading before my eyes. Zoltan is cursing up a storm, his arm wrapped around me in a crushing grip, as if that will somehow help Daren. Tenebris butts his head in my stomach and jolts me out of my fearful thoughts.

"If we get the book, he can stop fighting the magic coming from the portal." I have no idea if I'm right, but it's the best I have.

"Francesca." Saying my name as a warning, he tilts my face so I am forced to look at him. "Stay close to me. Promise."

"Fine, I promise. Let's go." When I try to step away, he heaves me back.

"Promise me." Staring at me intently, he doesn't move. "You can't help anyone if you get hurt."

"Don't you think I know that?" Hissing the words in frustration, I let him see my eyes change, the bright colors bursting to life almost blinding me. "Just get us close enough and I'll get the damn book back."

After searching my face, Zoltan stiffly nods before releasing his hold on me. A wolf yelps when a tendril grazes his muzzle, and I see him flinching back, snarling and baring his teeth. When Zoltan moves, I'm right next to him with Tenebris following at my back. It takes me by surprise when Zoltan's body expands, lifting him up until he towers over me enough to block the snapping wind. Changed into his true form, he glances down at me, the warning in those eyes clear. Before doing anything else, I gaze around him at Daren again.

Soren is holding one of the mage's hands, blood dripping from between their palms to the ground. The color is back on Daren's face, not by much but it's an improvement. It gives me hope that I'm not going to lose another person tonight. With renewed determination, I follow Zoltan as close as he dares to go without being slapped by twisting magic.

And then we wait.

Tenebris darts between two twisting lines, the green and blue smacking ominously close to his face. Jumping back, he roars loud enough to be heard over the wind. I watch the pattern of movement in hopes that I can find a way to dodge them and get to the book. Releasing the control on my magic, I feel my dragon unfurl inside me, too eager for another fight. My vision blurs for a second before each color of the magic coming at us from the portal separates, making it easier to track each movement.

I poke Zoltan, stabbing my finger in his hip.

"I can see them." Pointing at the tendrils, I try to step around him.

"No." A hand the size of my head with wicked claws pushes me back.

"You don't understand." Glaring at him, I'm stupefied when a bight glow frames his form. It's like an internal light has been flicked on and it radiates through his skin. Shaking my head, I file it away to examine later. "I can see them separated and can get us in. Please, you need to trust me."

It's a low blow because he knows that trust is important to me. I hate pulling that one on him, but I don't see another option. After a long moment, the hand holding me back disappears, and he nods as he steps to the side. Swallowing thickly, I take the lead and cross my fingers that I won't get us both killed. Placing all my weight on the balls of my feet, I hold my breath until I see the first opening.

Bolting for it, I feel both Zoltan and Tenebris close, and my adrenaline spikes because if they get any closer they'll trip me. It's a fleeting thought and it's gone quick, leaving me lost in snapping colors and repeating patterns. The three of us move back and forward, ducking, twisting, and jumping over the angry magic trying to slap us away. The power from the portal is stronger the closer we get, and it starts burning across my skin. Teeth clenched, I push on. I can see the figure holding the book much better now, and I'm shocked to see the familiar red hair and pale skin. Casius's daughter is the last person I expected back in Sienna.

Losing focus costs me.

An angry orange tendril of magic snaps across my chest and lifts me in the air. Searing pain ripples through my body, and for a split second I drift in and out of consciousness. Everything moves in slow motion as I float through the air, my braid flipping lazily around my head. Zoltan's hand latches onto my arm, and that brings reality back like the snapping of an elastic. My body is plucked from the air, turned upside down, and then plopped back on my feet. With a grunt, I lock my knees when they threaten to buckle.

"Let's go." Zoltan's voice drums in my chest like bass.

Tucking my chin closer to my chest, I push further. I get hit a few more times, but only because my mind can't believe who is helping Roberti destroy us all. With effort, I unclench my jaw so I don't grind my molars to dust. At the last three tendrils I stop, watching them erratically wriggle in front of my eyes.

"There is not enough of an opening," I call out to Zoltan over the roaring magic and wind. "I could pass … maybe. Or even Tenebris. No way you'll be able to go through." Not giving him a chance to stop me, I inch to the side. "Catch me if I fall."

And I pounce.

Chapter Nine

I feel weightless as I sail through the air, almost shouting in victory when I contour my back and pass the first two tendrils. Gravity tugs on me, pulling me lower than I intended until I see the last obstacle of magic, but it's a second too late. The color flares up, and if I didn't know better, I would think it's sentient and excited that there is no way for me to block it. It wriggles erratically like a snake pinned to the ground, sending my heart into tachycardia.

Then it snaps.

Pain like I've never felt before ripples across my torso and upper thighs, and I'm flung back with such force that my back collides with swirling magic from behind me. Roaring fills my ears, liquefying my brain as I'm being tossed between the tendrils like a pinball, each hit more painful than the next. A hand brushes against my arm, but it's gone the same second, Zoltan trying, and failing, to get a hold of me and pull me out. Everything blends together, and I feel my body giving up the fight without permission.

The pain is too much for me to even think, much less try to stop the momentum.

A black blur hits me from the side, the change in direction so abrupt that bile coats my throat like acid. I don't feel the impact with the hard ground because every inch of me is just one big ball of frayed nerve pain. A muscled body pins me underneath it, but I can't even cry out in pain. My mouth open in a silent scream, all I can do is take small sips of air. Any more than that and my chest will rip apart until all my insides spill out like a popped balloon.

Blinking fast, I clear my vision just enough to see smooth silky fur as Tenebris crouches over me, protecting my body with his own. Inching back, he brings his head close to my face, his eyes boring into mine as if he is trying to pierce my brain with his gaze. His upper lip curling, he bares his sharp teeth in my face, a low cry ripping from his chest.

I want to reassure him. I really do.

But all I can do is just stare back.

When Tenebris starts digging big chunks of dirt and grass from either side of me, I want to flinch, but I can't. His paws shovel it in every direction, some of it peppering over both of us. Panic seizes me that he is not himself, that maybe I already look dead and he's trying to bury my body. My eyes dart frantically around hoping to see Zoltan attempting to reach me, but the panther is obscuring my vision.

I see nothing but black fur and piercing eyes.

"No." Tears prickle my eyes when I move my lips, but the word is not even a whisper.

Raising his right paw above me, his glinting claws reflect the swirling colors around us as he swipes it down at my face. My eyelids squeeze shut and I brace for more pain. I don't even breathe when I feel the warm liquid raining all over my jaw and neck. Until I realize I didn't feel anything.

My eyes snap open.

Head tilted to the side, Tenebris is baring his neck, blood gushing from three claw marks on it bathing me in red. When I don't do what he expects, he lowers more and presses his throat to my face. My lips part from shock, and my mouth fills with his blood so fast I'm choking on it in no time. It doesn't faze him at all. Knowing I won't be able to breathe if I don't take what he offers, I gulp it down, each swallow burning like fire.

That's when I feel it.

My magic, which was drained from me while I was tossed around the flicking tendrils, roars to life. Like a beast that has been caged for too long against its will, it bursts through me so fast that, this time, I do scream. Every broken bone and torn muscle mends together at such a rapid pace I drift in and out of consciousness, my back bowed so much it almost dislodges Tenebris from me.

Zoltan's ferocious roar makes the ground shudder.

My power erupts, detonating out of me.

My ears pop from the pressure leaving me dazed but at least I'm not hurting anymore. Everything is blurry and distorted when I roll on my side and lift myself on shaking arms, panting for breath. The golden glow, which I assumed was just the magic lashing out of the portal, turns out to be a stream of power coming from my chest. It connects to the two pouring out of Daren's hands, thickening it and throwing sparkles everywhere.

Tenebris is the first to jump on all fours as he slinks to me, looking me up and down. Thankfully his neck is healed, although the fur is flattened and still wet down his chest. My mouth opens to say something to thank him, but I'm snatched in the air by two unforgiving hands, and then I'm flipped around to face Zoltan. His wild gaze searches every inch of me checking for injuries.

"I'm okay." Feet dangling, I croak out of a throat raw from screaming.

"I will kill you myself, Francesca." Snapping, he rattles my bones when he shakes me in anger.

"Oh goody, that's exactly what I wanted to hear after going through that shit." When his fingers tighten on me, I start wiggling. "Put me down, you ape, or she'll get away."

"I don't think she's going anywhere." The expression on his face tells me it hurts him to even talk to me right now. I was hoping to avoid telling him off until sometime later. Like next year or something.

Actually I was hoping I'd be dead so I could just avoid it.

Fuck my luck.

"Zoltan, just put me down ..." Grinding my teeth, I add a barely audible, "Please."

Eyes narrowed to slits, he lowers me to the ground so slow I want to scream at him, while suspicion and anger are twisting his features into a grimace. The two sharp points of his fangs poke out under his upper lip making him look ominous. As soon as the tips of my boots touch a solid surface, I yank my arms out of his hands and whirl to see what is left of the wide area around us.

Daren is leaning heavily on Leo, the alpha practically holding him up under his arm. The wolf is checking the mage's pulse, and his deep sigh shows me that he found it. Astara is nowhere to be seen, but I find her crouched next to half the body of Casius's daughter. I guess the portal cut her in two when it closed, giving me a whole new reason for freaking out when I need to go through it. The trepidation

71

in my gut eases a little when Astara lifts a hand holding the book in a white knuckled grip. Her too-wide gaze locks on mine over her shoulder and she nods as if I did something on purpose to help them.

All I did was get my ass handed to me by whoever the jerk was on the other side.

Tenebris leans on my thigh and my hand goes to his ear on its own. It brings me comfort just knowing the panther is there, no matter how much I give him grief for it. That's until my head moves away from Zoltan's sister and I find Soren.

A strangled sound chokes my throat.

I try to stop it, but I can't do it to save my life.

And I burst out laughing.

Soren's slinky hair is sticking out of his head as if he is standing next to a generator. Static is pulling the long strands into a huge halo around his stunned face. Dirt and what have you is smudged all over his bare arms and chest, as well as one side of his face. His silky pants are ripped to shreds and hanging off his hips in strips of fabric. It's unfair that, even like this, he still looks good enough to put the rest of us to shame. Well, except for the fact that he is glaring at me for laughing. That kind of ruins it for me.

"Do not taunt him." Zoltan steps closer to me, his arm going around my shoulders to pull me to his chest.

"Why?" Snorting ungracefully, I lean back and nestle against him. At least he is not pissed anymore. "He does look ridiculous."

Soren scowls at me, but I see the corners of his lips twitching.

"I think he is up to something." The murmur is for my ears only, and I do my best not to show a reaction.

"I think you are right." Looking down at Tenebris's

upturned face, I hide my lips so the ancient Fae can't read them.

"I need to check the portal and see what damage they did. Will you be okay?" Feeling the vibration in his chest when he speaks relaxes me further. He is alive, and so am I.

We can fight another day.

"I'll be fine. I need to check the infirmary." Watching Leo drag Daren toward the building, I push off Zoltan and follow them. "Hopefully Aspen made sure the creature was dead for real this time."

"I'll get the book and meet you there," Zoltan calls over his shoulder, already walking away to meet Astara at the portal.

I'm glad I don't have to go there. As much as I wanted to kill the redhead, I really don't want to look at her cut-up body. She got what she deserved. She is dead and we won a battle. No freeing Titans today for that asshole Roberti.

If only things were ever that easy.

Chapter Ten

I feel it the second my boots connect to the gravel. I almost reach the alpha and the mage, rushing to catch up with them. The magic keeping the place alive and protected reacts to the intrusion like a wild bull bucking under the weight of a rider trying to tame it. A ripple of revulsion and disgust passes through me, my own magic jumping to the surface and making me stumble forward. My arms shoot out to the sides so I don't lose my footing. Leo's head jerks in my direction, and even Daren opens his eyes wide as he struggles to straighten.

The portal makes a subtle popping sound, too loud in the sudden quiet.

"Leo, get her out of here." Zoltan's roar has me spinning on my foot and sprinting in his direction before he is done yelling, Tenebris right on my heels.

"Like hell you'll keep me away." Pushing the words through clenched teeth, my heart drops to my feet when I see the sea of hunters pouring out of the portal.

A feral cry comes out of Tenebris, and it pebbles my skin.

"Soren!" Screaming his name, my eyes search for the ancient Fae wildly as I pump my arms. When our gazes connect, I stab a finger in the direction of Zoltan. "The book!"

White noise fills my ears, the war beat of my heart muffled from it as I let go of the control I'm holding on my magic. I'll never admit this to anyone, not even if my life depends on it, but I'm scared of giving it full reign. There is a small part of me that refuses to be ruled by an ancient being that has a mind of its own—one that is separate from mine. I let it control my movements or actions but never fully my mind.

Until now.

Seeing Zoltan's body being swallowed by the hunters surrounding him and Astara breaks the fundamental leash I have on who I am and what I want to be. A new fear rears its ugly head. That male means so much to me. Is this the bond talking, or is it just me being a stupid female that has fallen hard for a male? The moment of truth I'm facing is this: there is no more Francesca Drake without Zoltan. I will die before I let anyone, including the Fates, take him from me.

A terrifying roar shakes the ground at my feet, shriveling my lungs in horror.

It came from me.

Tenebris, agile as the feline that he is, jumps to the side and away from me mid run. Colors burst to life around me, my vision sharpening enough to see the individual leaves on the trees and the thin veins spreading through them. Soren's joyful and excited laugh shouldn't surprise me, yet it does.

His grin grows unbelievably wide when I give him a sharp, narrow-eyed look.

"An sin tha thu, dràgon òg." Regally inclining his head —which should look ridiculous thanks to his long hair sticking out every which way—he lets his fingers transform into wicked-looking claws.

With a frown, I lift my hand in front of my face wiggling my own fingers. The wind is belting my face while magic pours out of the portal, so I have to work even harder to make any progress in my attempt to reach Zoltan and Astara. If he can do it, maybe I can too. Having no weapon but my own body, I force magic into my hands while hunters approach much faster than I want them to.

Nothing happens.

Disappointment is a bitter pill to swallow. The more bodies dressed in white that rush out through the swirling portal, the surer I am that we are all going to meet our end tonight. Even with Zoltan and Astara carving their way through hunters like swirling dervishes out on a mission. My gaze darts to the sky, seeing the large silver moon shining gently over us, her glittery rays weaving through the bright colors of life my dragon loves to see. *At least we will die on a pretty night*, I think stupidly to myself.

Sharp pain zaps through my shoulders and down my arms until they are numb. It ricochets to my neck and along my spine, taking my feet from under me. Not wanting to end up on my face, I tuck my head down while tilting my shoulder forward, using the momentum to roll for a few turns before bouncing up on my feet. When I pop right up, I'm not sure who is more surprised: me, or the hunter that stops before me with his eyes about to fall out of their sockets. My arm shoots out to grab him by the neck, but I stop short and my jaw hits my chest.

Claws.

Not just claws as wicked as Soren's, but the skin of my hand and arm is covered with a shimmering of tiny scales under a thin layer of my skin. Flexing my fingers, I dispassionately watch the hunter's head roll off his shoulders. My cheeks hurt from the huge smile on my face when I turn to the side and see Soren watching me with an emotion I cannot name in his too-old gaze.

"Tha iad ag iarraidh na tha agamsa. Chan eil mi a 'roinn, seann fhear." The sultry tone of my voice carries over the sound of the screams.

Guards are already streaking through the open space, some in human form and some in animal form, but all of them are attacking indiscriminately. White clothing is turning red, so much like the fury swirling through me painting my sight. I give Soren one last glance to ensure he is reading between the lines of what I just told him. Just in case, I repeat it for him in English.

"They want what I have." One of his perfect eyebrows cocks up when he hears me and the corners of his lips twitch. "I do not share, old man." When mirth dances in his ancient eyes, I offer him a humorless smile, clarifying it for him. "Not even with you. Do not test me."

Taken aback, he gives a barely perceptible nod.

That's all I need … for now.

Clearing a path to Zoltan is much easier with my new dagger fingers. Tenebris is still keeping a safe distance between us, but he doesn't leave my side. With Soren making bodies fly left and right as if a tornado is passing through them, I focus on my mate. Zoltan's eyes glow brighter when they zero in on me, as if he somehow has heard my thoughts.

My arm protests from the burning when a star covered

in poison slices through my skin, opening it to the bone. Hand dropping limply to my side, I grind my teeth when my magic churns in my chest before rushing to the injury and repairing it instantly. No trace of the poison is left within seconds, and that leaves me stunned.

With renewed vigor I dance around hunters, spinning, kicking, and slicing through them like butter. Between their pathetic attempts to hurt us, I see Zoltan's body healing in a similar way. Something to ask him about after we make it out of here alive. The more we kill doesn't put a damper in their numbers, though. More just keeping coming, replacing the ones lying dead on the ground. We have to close the portal even while we continue fighting for our lives.

"Soren." Shouting while twisting away from a dagger, I kick a hunter in his teeth and send him toppling over. He takes four others down with him. "I'll help them. You close the portal. We can't fight them all."

Soren's eyebrows crawl up his forehead, and he jerks his chin at something over my shoulder before continuing with his fighting, graceful like a fucking gazelle in the midst of all the carnage. Craning my neck, I almost laugh when I see Argoz in his ghoul form with a full horde of shifters, mages, and demons at his back, wedging a path to join us.

Zoltan's ferocious bellow warns me at the last moment.

I jerk my head straight.

Two hunters block my path, one of them kicking dirt and upturned soil in my face. A tiny pebble smacks me in the corner of my eye, making it water and my vision blurry.

That's when I remember the serpentine stone in my pocket.

Since I promised it to Myst, I've been carrying it around in case I see her. Knowing the affect it has on me, I rip out my pocket with my claws to reach it, unable to shove my hand inside. It falls in my palm as I notice Zoltan fighting his way to me with less finesse. Ducking, I pull the chain over my head and lock gazes with him.

"Take it off me when it's over."

His shout and Tenebris's cry are drowned in the thundering that takes over my mind. A spike of fear is all I feel before coldness sweeps through my veins, icing my blood. My teeth chatter for a long second as I watch everything around me move in slow motion. My heartbeat slows until it fully stops. Somewhere deep in the back of my mind I'm aware that this is not good. Yet I stand still, even as daggers come at my neck from every side.

A black streak through the air shows Tenebris taking down the hunter on my right, his jaws clamping around the abomination's throat and ripping it out. Blood gushes down the panther's chin while he shakes his head from side to side. Frozen in place, my mouth opens in a desperate attempt to ... do what exactly? Breathe? Scream? I have no idea myself.

Then everything stops.

Dust moths flicker through the air like dancing pixies, reflecting the colors of life around me. Faces twisted in anger, pain, and determination meet my eye everywhere I turn. My gums burn and my fangs drop until they pierce my lower lip. That one drop of blood that wells up before trickling down my lip and jaw is like the answer to everything I want but never dared ask for.

An inferno bursts at the center of my chest.

A battle cry is ripped from my throat when my body turns to fire.

I'm standing in the center of blinding rage, eager to feed on all that have wronged me.

And I move.

The screams, pained roars, and shouts are muted while my eyes are trained on Zoltan. My body is contouring in ways I didn't think possible, avoiding weapons and flying shuriken faster than any vampire I've ever seen. Curling my claws into my palms, I shred my skin and allow my blood to flow freely down my hands. It leaves a trail at my feet, and the earth soaks it up greedily. That's when Soren's lifeforce links to mine. I feel it as a foreign thing that shouldn't be there. When I try to resist it, it sinks its proverbial hooks into me and I have no way of kicking it out.

Magic pours out of me in waves, smacking every one of the hunters left standing to the ground. My body turns on its own and I face the portal, the spinning, sparkling colors becoming transparent. Unfortunately for me (yet very fortunate for him) I see Roberti standing on the other side, his face pale and mouth gaping.

A smile curls my lips, and he takes a step back.

Zoltan steps behind me before his hand wraps around my shoulder. The usual heat of his body feels like a chilly breeze on my back, which is a startling sensation but not an unwelcome one. What is not good to see is the wriggling shadow next to Roberti. It isn't separate from him, either. No, it's like the two of them are one being residing in two different dimensions. It's the same one I saw what feels like a lifetime ago on the streets of Sienna as it devoured people until nothing remained of them.

"It was him all along," I tell Zoltan, not recognizing my own voice.

"I will die before he hurts you." Voice rough and too deep, he pulls me closer to his chest.

I snicker.

"Tha mi a 'tighinn air do shon. Thathas a 'gabhail ris

80

an dùbhlan agad." My words brim with power and echo in the sudden silence surrounding us.

I know Roberti hears me because he takes another step back, his knees bending in a fighting stance. That's when I realize he can't see me. And that I haven't felt my heartbeat for longer than I should.

"Francesca?" Zoltan sounds wary, but his hand is steady on my shoulder.

"I'm coming for you." Curling my claws over Zoltan's hand, I make sure Roberti hears the promise in my voice. I don't want him having any doubts that his end is near, and that it will come by my hand. "Your challenge is accepted, fucker."

There is a tug on my neck, and I twist to glance at Zoltan a second before all the strength leaves me. In his other hand, the chain of my necklace is dangling, the serpentine stone swaying like a pendulum. My body sags on him heavily as I gasp for air, and then my heart takes a hard, painful beat.

Thump.

"I got you." Zoltan scoops me in his arms and my fingers tipped with claws brush against Tenebris where my arm is hanging limply down.

Thump.

The fire drains from me in a whoosh that turns me into a wet noodle with the mother of all headaches. Soren's face pops into my line of sight, his brows puckering in a frown.

"The book?" Rasping, I hope to hear we didn't lose it.

"Safe," the ancient Fae mumbles as he watches me thoughtfully.

"Astara?" Gasping my friend's name, I cling to consciousness with everything I have. "Feed her my blood."

"No." There is no room left for argument in Zoltan's snap.

"Feed her—" A cough rakes my body, and I curl like a fetus against his chest.

"I will feed her my blood, young dragon." Soren sounds too far away. "You did well protecting what you have claimed as your own." I must be imagining the sadness in his voice.

He keeps talking, but darkness tugs on my mind and I eagerly rush into its embrace.

Chapter Eleven

"Did we lose a lot of people?" Tugging the covers closer around me, I watch Zoltan stoically regarding me from the foot of the bed.

I think Aspen is still freaked about drugging him and chaining him to the bed because she doesn't stop Zoltan when he says he is taking me out of the infirmary. I wake up there feeling like death has ran over me, so I can't protest too much when he plucks me out of the bed and walks out without a second glance. The feisty redhead nurse is too eager to assist him as well, much to my dismay. And then I'm in Zoltan's bed, only this time the others aren't here to help me deflect.

"Ten." The vampire was unnaturally still as his intense, unreadable gaze rooted on mine. "Considering there were over a hundred or so hunters, we didn't lose many."

"How many is too many, Zoltan?" Getting more apprehensive the longer he stares at me, I fidget on the bed. "In case you didn't notice, Roberti is upping his game. We were sure he couldn't get his hands on the book, yet we kept it here by pure luck."

"Luck had nothing to do with it." Cocking his head slightly to the side, he narrows his eyes. "What happened back there, Francesca? I felt your anger through the bond and the next thing I know our connection was overwhelmed by fury like I've never felt before."

My mouth opens and closes a few times, but no words come out. How do I explain the face that I gave full control to the creature inside me? Zoltan, just like Soren and Fenrir, has asked me to do that many times, but looking at it from this new perspective, I'm not sure they had any idea what they were asking of me. Ever since I discovered I have a sentient being sharing my body I've seen us as two separate beings. What happened in that open space in front of the portal left me unsettled and more scared that I've ever been before.

We were one.

Me and the creature I fear so much.

My thoughts were her thoughts, and her actions were my actions. How do I explain this to him without admitting I'm something that shouldn't exist? No one should hold that much power.

No one.

Yet here I am in the middle of the people I grew to care about, barely a girl in my near thirties compared to the centuries they've all lived, with enough power to hold their lives in the palm of my hand. The moment all the hunters dropped on the ground was when everything became crystal clear. I chose to have the rest protected from my magic. It was a conscious decision on my part. I could've easily been the only one standing in that open field otherwise. With the exception of Soren ... maybe. I'm still not sure he would've survived either.

Mind spinning with everything I should say but wouldn't, I watch Zoltan move around the bed. The mattress dips when he sits gently to my right, taking my hand in his. Warmth spreads from my fingers up my arm simply from being connected to him. Where our skin touches, a tingling sensation remains, reminding me he can feel my emotions. My gaze jerks from his chest to his face.

"I don't know." My answer to his question is barely a breath passing my lips.

"Talk to me." Holding me prisoner in those blue eyes of his, he rubs his thumb over the back of my hand. The movement is curiously soothing, and hypnotic. "I have lived long enough and have probably seen it all. Do not shut me out. I felt your panic. Allow me to share the burden of whatever it is."

"Astara will be okay?"

"She will be fine." The smirk I'm all too familiar with tells me he knows I'm deflecting. "As will Leo, Daren, Soren, and Argoz, too. Anyone else's wellbeing you'd like to know about?"

"I would've asked about my mother, but she is enjoying life in ignorance back in Sienna where we left her after her disastrous dinner with that jerk Silas." My drawl has enough snark to make one corner of his full lips twitch.

"Share with me." The amusement leaves his face as he tugs gently on my hand.

"I had claws." That's the first thing I blurt out like an idiot.

"It was hard not to notice." Another twitch of his lips, but his gaze stays steadily locked on mine, which tells me we'll be sitting here until I spill all my secrets. No matter how long I take to do it.

So, I tell him everything. Because my heartbeat is in my throat, the words come out rushed and choked, but the longer I speak the easier it gets. By the time I'm done I am exhausted, both mentally and physically. My body sags deeper into the mattress and pillows, a bone-weary sigh ending my confession.

"You've released the control before," Zoltan repeats that twice as if saying it more than once will make it true.

"No, I haven't." Closing my eyes when his fingers brush away stray hairs from my face makes it easier to admit things. If I don't see him, he can't see me, which is my type of stupidity. "There was always a part of me that had some control so I could get back to myself. Even the first time in the woods when we were returning from the human realm and I was climbing trees delivering silent deaths, I knew deep down I could come back to Francesca Drake if I wanted. Not this time."

"You are always Francesca Drake. Difference is you were afraid this time." At my sharp glare, he backpedals fast. "For *my* life, since so many hunters coming through the portal. We went through something similar not long ago and I was taken," he clarifies with an arrogant curl to his mouth. My hand is itching to slap it off his handsome face. "Add to that worry for Astara's life, as well as the book. You like to talk a tough game, but Daren is still your friend and seeing him draining his life to hold the portal worried you, too. Losing the connection with Fenrir left you emotionally wide open for extremes. I like and admire your feisty spirit, but I do love your kind heart. Don't debate it with me, I feel you through the bond."

"Lo and behold, Zoltan the philosopher. They'll build

you a monument in the middle of Sienna one of these days." When his eyebrows pucker in a frown, I snicker. "I'll make sure I egg it when it happens. To give it more of a rustic feel, you know."

"You shouldn't fear yourself." Ignoring my smartass comments, he continues watching me steadily. Heat creeps up my cheeks under the scrutiny. "Letting go of control is the only way of having it."

"What if it overtakes me?" Voicing the greatest fear I have, my lips tremble. I know he can hear my heart punching my ribs like there is no tomorrow. "What if I lose myself in that much power, Zoltan? It's addictive to know you hold anyone's life in your hand. That you can end their existence with just a flick of your fingers. We are not gods. We shouldn't be."

"We are not gods," he agrees, crawling on the bed and pulling me over his lap. "But we might as well be. Now that you've seen the humans yourself, you understand why we are behind these portals. Why we must keep our presence in their realm minimal and monitored. To them we are gods who hold their lives in the palm of our hand."

"Roberti—"

"And why we must use any advantage we have to stop Roberti." He talks over me, cutting off whatever I was about to say. "Anyone can get drunk on too much power, love. That's why you have me." Tucking his chin to his chest, he peers down at my upturned face. "The reason you felt like you did was because you weren't expecting it. Neither did I. It was too much magic, too fast, and with no warning. I think I can help you balance it out."

"You don't sound too sure of your own claims." The steady beat of his heart—which I still find strange since it wasn't there the first time he held me like this—calms me.

"I am not." His eyes stay locked on mine for a long moment of silence before he speaks again. "For you I am willing to try. For you, Francesca Drake, I am capable of much worse things than Roberti." A lump forms in my throat, and I blink fast to stop the prickling tears from spilling down my cheeks. "To have that much power over a creature like me makes you one of the gods you fear becoming."

"This is not helping." The words come out in a croak, so I clear my throat. "I don't want that much power."

"And that's exactly why I am sure you will never lose yourself in it." Kissing the top of my head, he leans back and closes his eyes. "If anyone should have it, I am very happy to know that it's you."

"Did you know?"

"Did I know what? That you are that powerful?" One of his eyes pops open to look down at me.

"About the oath Fenrir took to bond himself to me." Until this moment, I never knew how much it bothered me to know this.

"I knew about him taking the oath, but not to whom. By the time I found out, it was a little too late to go back on what I was doing."

"What do you mean?"

"When I saw you the first time and started following you around to make sure you didn't get hurt, I didn't know you were the Dragon Blood. By the time I knew it for sure, I was already willing to protect you with my life."

"That's why you and Fenrir postured from day one like peacocks?"

"The fairy didn't stand a chance." Using my insult for Fenrir, Zoltan chuckles deep when I thump my fist on his chest.

"You didn't know that, you arrogant ass. I could've told you to fuck off."

"You could've, Ms. Drake." I squeak when he flips me around and pins me under him. "Yet here you are in my bed."

"Who's deflecting now?" Forcing myself to ignore the fact that his lips are so close they are brushing mine when I talk, I keep eye contact. "You hid that from me."

"I couldn't say anything because I didn't understand it." A line slices the middle of his forehead and pulls his eyebrows low over his eyes. "How could I feel you as mine if you had a bond with someone else. I was afraid to ask any information about it at the time."

"You? Afraid?"

"Very." He grins at me, but the concern and confusion still linger in his gaze.

"Who would you ask?"

"Soren." As soon as the name passes Zoltan's lips there is a knock on the door, the energy rolling off the person preceding the one that wields it.

Speak of the devil.

"I hope you are both decent because I'm coming in," the ancient Fae announces before waltzing inside as if he owns the room.

Chapter Twelve

Zoltan stays on top of me, his smirk getting more frustrating as the seconds tick by. I wriggle uncomfortably underneath him. Glaring doesn't help, either. In fact, it only makes him grin like the cat that ate the canary, and I resort to childish actions. Example: kneeing him to get him to move. Rolling off me, his dark chuckle does stupid things to my body, and I try to ignore those things even though it takes great effort on my part. The male is so arrogant it'll take a whole planet falling on top of his head to take him down a notch. Pointedly avoiding looking at Soren, I scoot up the bed and pull the covers over me like a shield.

"The book is secure I take it?" Soren gives Zoltan a barely-there nod as an answer to his question, but he keeps his slanted gaze glued on me.

"How was Roberti able to open the portal the way he did?" Not giving the ancient Fae time to start interrogating me, I turn everyone's attention to what happened in the field.

"We already know he has a very powerful mage working

with him, do we not?" Keeping his unwavering gaze on me, Soren moves languidly around the room with one long finger trailing over the couple of pieces of furniture in it. "As much as Casius would love to name himself as such, this is not him. The flavor is not right. It's older ... much older."

"Could it be the shadow he had with him?" Saying it out loud pebbles my skin and turns my stomach inside out.

"We do not know what, or who he had with him." The way Soren says that irritates me to no end. Like I'm a youngling who is telling him tales.

"We know the shadow was there." I wouldn't be Franky Drake if I didn't rise to the challenge, so I speak slowly as if he is stupid.

Soren's face, which was finally pointed at the window instead of on me, snaps in my direction, a slight glow burning in the depths of his eyes.

"We do?" The intensity of his scrutiny makes me squirm.

"Both of you were there. You saw it." Looking at Zoltan for confirmation is a bad idea.

The confusion plastered on his handsome face is replacing the smirk, and alarms that blare in my head at that. Soren leans his upper body forward as if I'm about to tell them the greatest secret of all ages, and that is not helping matters either. With doubt clouding my judgment, I try to recall what I saw across the portal. Roberti's leering, twisted face blanched of all color as he took one step back, then another floats to the front of my mind. Was I so out of it at the end of that fight that I imagined the whole thing? Or was I really losing myself to all the magic and power inside me and it made me hallucinate? Was he even really there?

"What did you see, young dragon?" Platinum hair

trickles over Soren's shoulder like someone is pouring paint over him when he glides across the room to stand across from Zoltan on the other side of the bed.

I need to get up.

Having both imposing males looming over me on either side creates panic, and it claws at my chest. Like a cornered animal, my eyes dart around the room looking for an escape that I know I'll never get to. Not with the speed these two are capable of. I still try.

Bouncing off the bed, I bolt for the door, but Soren blocks my way by materializing in front of me as if he always stood there. Changing direction, I head for the window, but a second later two strong arms wrap around my waist and I'm lifted from the ground. My rational mind left me the second the doubt set in, so my gums are throbbing, my fangs biting into my lower lip as I try to claw my way out of Zoltan's embrace.

Pure insanity.

I kick, twist, and rake my nails over his forearms to no avail. Dark blood covers my fingers where Zoltan's skin breaks, tiny rivulets of it trailing down and dripping over the carpeted floor. Jerking my head to the side, I sink my fangs in his upper arm and tug like a feral beast caught in a trap. He grunts but doesn't let go, his hold tightening further as he presses me to his chest. When my magic perks in reaction to my fight or flight instinct, Zoltan's body disappears from my back and I find myself pinned on the floor staring wide eyed at the ceiling. My gaze automatically goes to the spot I know has a removable tile—the same spot the book was hidden until not long ago.

"Breathe." Soren's mesmerizing, lyrical voice penetrates the hysteria pushing me to run.

I must run.

I need to hide.

It's too much.

Pressure like the entire earth is pressing on my chest forces me to gasp and take a breath.

"Breathe, young dragon," the ancient Fae coos at me. "Just breathe."

Sucking in deep breaths like a drowning woman helps clear the haze that is attempting to take over my mind, the blurry shapes around me become clear and the dark spots at the corners of my eyes disappear when my lungs get much-needed oxygen. White noise thunders in my ears but gets fainter the longer I'm on the floor.

"I'm going insane." My words are barely understandable since they are spoken through gulping air. "I need to be put down."

"Stop talking nonsense, child. Just focus on your breathing. All will be well. Just breathe." Soren doesn't move from his spot above me.

As I'm slowly calming from my panic attack, I notice that the ancient Fae is not touching me in any way. His right hand is making lazy circles at his side, but apart from that, not a muscle moves. Standing just to the side, he is focused on me with a slight line between his brows, which is the only indicator of the effort he is putting in. That, more than anything else subsides me. If Soren can control me when I'm out of my mind, there may be hope.

"She believes that she is losing herself to her Dragon Blood." Zoltan's voice is strained as he moves closer so I can see him.

I cringe when my eyes travel along his arms where skin is healing from claw marks. *My* claw marks from when I tried to escape. As if reading my mind, he looks down at me, one side of his lips twitching in amusement.

"It'll take more than a few scratches for me to let you go, love." Heat pools in my belly from the husky tone in his voice and the hunger in his gaze. "This I call foreplay." With a cocky smirk, he lifts both arms proudly showing them to Soren like he has won an award.

I glare at him.

"I shouldn't worry about going insane. All of us are nuts here." With an ungraceful snort, I try to roll to my side with no result. "Let me go, Soren. I'm not going to attack either of you."

The doubtful look contouring his too-pretty face makes me want to slap him. After a staring match that lasts too long, he stops moving his hand and all the pressure holding me down disappears. Zoltan's dark chuckle when I scramble to my feet earns him an elbow to the ribs.

"Let us hear about what you can see through a closed portal." Soren must be high or drunk if he thinks I'll let him get away with shit.

"You've been holding out on us." Squaring off with him, I fold my arms across my chest to hide the tremble I still have lingering there, but the two arrogant males don't need to know that.

"How so?" The innocent expression on the ancient Fae's face looks so out of place that it's comical.

"If you have that much power, why didn't you do more when we needed you?" When his forehead puckers, I clench my fists. "People died in that field, Soren. To you that might not be a big deal, but if you could have prevented it, you should have. It is your duty to do so instead of playing games."

Power hits me so sudden and hard I stumble back a few steps before catching myself. Zoltan hunches his shoulders with his fangs bared, ready to tackle the Dragon Blood that is glaring daggers my way. It's hard to breathe even without having your lungs seared from the density of magic saturating the air and prickling my skin.

"How dare you lecture me on duty." The deceptively low tone of his words is the scariest thing I've ever heard.

"You could've ended that fight without straining a muscle." Stubbornly I hold on to my accusations, swallowing my heart because it's trying to punch its way out through my throat. "I knew you were selfish but this goes beyond anything I could've dreamed off. These people count on you to protect them and keep them safe. Isn't that what you signed up for?"

"Protecting them is your job now, young dragon. Do not pass the mantle so soon." Mocking me, he smiles, but there is no humor in it.

"You could've saved them—"

"Francesca." Zoltan's warning passes through one ear and out the other.

"You chose to let them die. Those lives are on you, and no amount of mocking and gloating will change that. You sacrificed lives for your ideals and arrogance." Spitting the words in disgust, I look away from him.

"I sacrificed lives?" Soren laughs humorlessly. "You are sacrificing an entire species, Francesca Drake." Hissing my name like a curse, he gets in my face. "Let us talk about duty, shall we?"

"Oh, dear Fates you are still going on about that damn bond? The one that, need I remind you, I never agreed to with Fenrir?" Stepping closer to him, I bump our noses together, the anger boiling inside me ready to spill over. "I am not a broodmare, Soren. You like to blame the bond I have with Zoltan, but even without it, I would've never agreed to any of the plans you tried to force on me."

"You are a Dragon Blood." Not stepping down, he speaks as if that should explain everything.

Red clouds my vision and I bare my fangs at him.

"I am also a vampire!" Some little box Zoltan has on his chest of drawers rattles from my roar.

A hard thump makes the door to the room groan on the frame. All three of us spin in that direction, spreading out and taking positions to fight whatever it is that's trying to break its way in. And break it does a second later when splinters and larger pieces of wood spray in all directions as the door bursts as if hit by a bomb. A dark shape blurs around us so fast none of us have time to react, at least until Soren ends up pinned on the wall with a very pissed-off panther holding the Fae's throat between his sharp teeth.

Standing on his hind legs, Tenebris is almost as tall as me, which places his deadly choppers at the perfect height to rip Soren's neck to smithereens. I was wondering where the shifter was when I woke up in the infirmary, but with all the guilt and fear riding my ass, I didn't ask or give it a second thought. Obviously, he wasn't too far. The sounds coming through his wide-open jaw are raising the short hairs on the back of my neck as saliva drips down Soren's still-bare chest.

The male needs a shirt.

Nailed to his torso so he can't take it off.

"The loyalty you inspire in others is astonishing, young dragon. Even the mighty Tenebris is acting like your house pet. The Fates must have tied him to you and wherever your destiny leads, to have him be so protective of you and offer his life for yours in every turn." A small smile dances on his bow-shaped lips while he ignores the deadly teeth clamped around his throat.

Tenebris snarls.

"Let him go, Tenebris." With a sigh, I rub a hand over my face.

All the anger and panic from earlier leaves me drained, and I stagger to the bed slumping on it. Soren is an asshole. Selfish, arrogant, maybe even a little crazy, but I don't want him dead. I just want him to get his head out of his ass and start working with us instead of chasing pipe dreams and his own agendas. Whatever they may be. And after that display of power earlier when he pinned me to the floor with just a twirl of his hand, I have a feeling my friend will get hurt before he has a chance to harm the ancient Fae.

Soren is playing with all of us like we are mice in a cage built for his entertainment.

It needs to stop.

"Let him go." Repeating my request, I reach a hand toward Tenebris, who is giving me a narrowed look from one eye, his jaw still around the Fae. "He is a jerk, and insufferable, but not the enemy. We do need his help."

If a panther can look doubtful, that's the expression on Tenebris's face right now. He snarls once more at Soren before pushing off him none too gently. Zoltan snorts, covering it with a cough when the shifter hisses at him. Felines, big or small, really are very temperamental. Prowling like the predator that he is, the panther comes to my side, killing his tough vibe by starting to purr the second my fingers start scratching behind his ears.

Zoltan throws his head back and laughs.

Even Soren chuckles, shaking his head.

I find no humor in any of it.

"Let's talk, Soren." With another sigh, I curl my legs under me, Tenebris jumping on the bed and cuddling at my side with one eye open so he can watch the Fae. "I need to explain a few things to you so we can put this whole "continuing the line" bullshit to rest once and for all."

Chapter Thirteen

"I'm not sure how long you've been sleeping and ignoring the world around you." The blank look on his face drowns me in sadness and guilt, but I push on, determined to get to the bottom of this. "Half-bloods have always been an abomination meant to be gotten rid of, and they never stay alive long enough for anyone to see if they could be more. Some are in hiding like I was, but even then, one thing has been a constant throughout our history." Raising a hand, I stop whatever Zoltan is about to say. "Zoltan, I've come to terms with it more or less. No need for reassurances. The point I'm trying to make here for Soren is this: there has never been an offspring from a half blood. The Fates didn't find us worthy of continuing our lines, Dragon Bloods or not."

The silence that follows my words—words I've pushed so deep to the back of my mind I never thought I'd think them much less say them out loud—is oppressing. Avoiding looking at the two males because I don't want to see their pity, which will be worse than anything else they can offer at the moment, I stare unseeing through the window, the darkness outside matching my mood. My fingers trailing over the smooth soft fur down Tenebris's neck and spine, I sigh.

"There's one other thing I learned growing up too. We can't form bonds or find a true mate."

Zoltan clears his throat.

"The connection between us is strong." Offering him a small smile to take away the sting of my words, I drop my gaze to my lap. "More than I ever wished or dreamed of for sure. A true-mate bond though … well, it's not. I've accepted it, and I'm grateful for it, though I can't help but wonder if this is not some bond forged from oaths or what have you." Peeking at Soren through my lashes, I'm too afraid to ask. But I do it anyway. "It's not, right? This thing between us"—Flicking a hand between Zoltan and me, I see the vampire scowl from the corner of my eye—"isn't one of your parlor tricks like with Fenrir, is it?"

"I did not have anything to do with your bond, if that is what you are asking." The ancient Fae leans back on the wall behind him, tucking his hands in the pockets of the tactical pants he found to replace his silky ones, oblivious to the glistening drool Tenebris left on his neck and chest. "However, I cannot say I agree with the rest of your facts."

"I'm not sure how to break it to you, old man, but just because you don't want to hear it doesn't mean it's not the truth. Even if I agreed to that insane idea to make babies with Fenrir…" At Zoltan's deep, menacing snarl, I can't help but snicker—"It's just an *if* scenario to humor Soren, so calm your tits. Anyway, if that *was* an option, I'm telling you that you'd have been sorely disappointed."

"Shall I be the one to tell her?" Soren's tone jerks my head up and I narrow my eyes at his contemplative face. "Or will you do the honors, Zoltan?"

"What are you talking about?" Apprehension causes bile to burn the back of my throat.

Zoltan stills where he is standing, a muscle jumping on one side of his jaw while he glares at Soren. My head swivels from one to the other, getting confused by the vampire's building anger and the smile growing on Soren's face.

"What?" Snapping at both of them, I make Tenebris hiss in frustration.

"What do you know about mates, young dragon?" Basking in the attention he craves like an addict craving a drug of choice, the Fae looks as happy as a pig in mud. "I'm sure your mother has told you tales. Let us hear them."

"That you recognize them the second you lay eyes on them, and it's a connection so strong neither can resist it. It's a perfect match the Fates create, and they don't leave it to chance. The bond snaps into place and will keep the two together for eternity."

"Indeed." Soren looks pointedly from me to Zoltan. I ignore the wild beating of my heart and the numbness that starts spreading from the tips of my fingers up my arms. "What else?"

"There was no bond snapping in place between the two of us." Even I can hear the conviction lacking in my words.

"Let us not think on that now. What else?" If Soren keeps smiling that wide, I honestly think his face will split in half.

"After the bond forms they will do anything to stay close to each other until they seal it—"

"How?" the Fae cuts me off, which earns him a glare. "Seal it how?"

"Exchange of blood, physical connection ..." my words

trail off and I stare at Zoltan's profile. He won't look at me. "We didn't exchange blood for the longest time."

The expression on Soren's face calls me an idiot.

I am an idiot.

"I can't form a true-mate bond." Reverting to my old argument, I lift my chin stubbornly.

"Do you know anything else about mates?" Ignoring my comment, Soren is practically vibrating from happiness. The asshole loves being one step ahead of me at all times.

"No." Tired of the bullshit, I give up on playing this stupid game. "Why don't you enlighten me, oh wise one."

"I thought you'd never ask." I regret my last words when he shoves off the wall, waving his hands excitedly while he talks.

Zoltan hasn't moved a muscle.

"What you said is true, and yet not enough. You see, young dragon, when two mates meet, the instinct to show they are capable of protecting each other comes full force. All oaths and honor bound promises are forgotten."

"Tell that to Fenrir," I point out, but he dismisses my smartass remark with a flick of his wrist. A memory of Zoltan picking me up when I came to this damn place and the portal was attacked silences whatever else I am going to say.

"He fought it, so I must give him respect for that, but it's a fight that no one can win." Ignorant to my stunned expression, the gloating slips from Soren's face and his forehead wrinkles slightly in a frown that doesn't last long. "Many have fought the bond, but all lose the battle. In those cases, the mates still try to give or take blood."

My eyes dart to Zoltan, remembering the evening when he offered his wrist to me, which ensured I never looked at that window on the third floor the same way. Butterflies erupt in my stomach to this day when I pass by it. I eagerly took his offer, not even resisting much. I'm well aware of how selfish vampires are with their blood because I'm the same way myself when it comes to it, but he had a good argument. He was only trying to help, nothing else. If I say it a couple more times maybe I'll start believing it.

"Wherever you see one, the other is never too far away. And when one is in danger, the other will go to great lengths to keep them safe. Logic does not prevail in that. They also show their true forms to each other."

Soren stops pacing and turns to Zoltan folding his arms across his chest. The vampire might as well not be here because he hasn't blinked from the moment this conversation started. The fact that I didn't think twice in our attempt to go through the hunters and get to the portal before allowing my Dragon Blood to take over around Zoltan is like one more nail in my pounding head.

"How long has it been since you've been in your true form, Zoltan? Before the battle for taking over the Order, I should say." Soren sounds too innocent to pull off being curious.

Zoltan says nothing.

Dread pools in my stomach.

"I believed you locked your true form, just as you gave up your mate bond when you took an oath to protect our world, as well as the human's." With an ambiguous shrug, the Fae pretends like what he just said is not a big deal. "So, knowing all this leads us to the important issue we are facing."

I don't want to hear the important issue.

I don't even want to know there is anything to deal with other than the hunters we are facing.

Those I can fight and kill.

"I was wrong." Hearing those words coming out of Soren's mouth silences everything else churning in my head.

"I'm sorry, what?" I meant it as a question, but it came out in a shout.

"I know it should not have happened." Slicing a hand through the air, the Fae looks stunned. "I have not been mistaken on anything, but you, young dragon, are defying the laws of nature and the rules of the Fates. Which leads me to the second most important fact."

Don't say it! My mind is screaming but nothing passes my numb lips. I'm not sure I'm even breathing, the room around me swaying like I'm sitting on a boat as I hear Soren's voice coming from a great distance away.

"You can continue your bloodline. Of this I am certain." To make matters worse, he turns to Zoltan proudly and doesn't stop talking. "But you knew that, Blood King. Am I correct on that, too?"

The world around me stops.

The time since I've known Zoltan plays in fast forward at the front of my mind like a movie. The bond we have and how it came to be. Every time I turn around seeing him just a few feet away, following behind like a shadow no matter how pissed I was at him. Slinking around the building searching for him and hoping he would not notice. How much I fought my attraction to him, yet like moth to a flame I couldn't stay away. And the worst of all, the fact that, at the moment, he is blocking the bond so I can't tell what he is feeling.

Slowly I push off the bed and jump to my feet. With measured steps, I tiptoe around pieces of the broken door and exit the room without either one of them trying to stop me. At the threshold I halt, not turning around. I'm not sure I want to see the look on Zoltan's face right now.

"Did you know all this time?" I don't have to tell them who I'm asking even with my voice coming out barely above whisper.

"Only a blind fool wouldn't know," the Fae chirps without being asked to make a comment.

The silence following Soren's words lasts too long.

"Yes," Zoltan answers after an eternity just as softly.

My braid slaps my back and shoulders as I run through the hallways. Tears prickle my eyes, but I don't let them fall. They are out of anger and betrayal more than anything else. At least that's what I tell myself. People I pass act alert as if expecting another attack, but I just don't have it in me to tell them it's an attack on my sanity and heart. A foe I can't fight no matter how much I want to.

So, I run.

Maybe trying to escape myself.

Passing the large double doors of the entrance, I jump over the few steps to the ground, my bare feet scraping over the pebbles. It stings but I barely notice it. Without turning I know Tenebris is behind me, wisely keeping his distance but not letting me out of his sight. The shifter can't even talk, so I shouldn't be angry at him. The problem is that I'm angry at everything and everyone right now. With no destination in mind, my feet pound on the ground, my arms pumping until a stitch develops in my side. I stop in the middle of the woods, dropping on my knees and gasping for air.

That's when I allow the tears to fall.

Hands pressed on my thighs, my body rocks from the gut-wrenching sobs that are ripped from my chest. Bending forward, I press my forehead to the ground and let every-thing I've bottled inside come out in ugly, loud cries, not caring if anyone can hear me. Tenebris's presence taunts me from between the trees, but he stays hidden to give me space. What feels like a lifetime later, when my eyes are dry, I roll limply on my side and stretch on the forest floor staring numbly at the sky.

"Did it make you feel better?" Astara's voice reaches my ears, but I don't have the strength to turn my head and look at her. I didn't even feel someone else coming near.

"No."

"I didn't think so." Rocks crunch under her feet as she approaches me, plopping down on the ground next to my head. "I tried it too the other day. It just gave me a headache." With a sigh, she lays down mimicking me, her arm brushing mine as she settles.

"Zoltan knew we had a true-mate bond." My voice cracks and I clear my throat, which feels raw from crying so long. "Did you?"

"I hoped it was." The words come out soft, and I can see her turning her head to look at the side of my face. "I've never seen my brother bat an eye about a female until you came along. Knowing he had to sacrifice it for the oath made me see it as wishful thinking."

"You heard the conversation?" How else would she know what I'm talking about?

"I was coming to check on you." Turning her gaze back to the treetops and the sky, she giggles nervously. "I tried to walk away when I heard what you were talking about, but I couldn't get my feet to move. You could say I eavesdropped." Bumping her elbow on mine, this time she does snicker with humor. "What are friends for if not to hear things you don't want them to so they can make fun of you later?"

"There is nothing funny about this, Astara." Tenebris must've decided it was safe to come out because he lays down on my other side, pretending not to look at me.

"Would it be so bad?" Her question is tentative and barely audible.

"Would what be bad?"

"To have a youngling." Bile like acid burns the roof of my mouth from her question.

"Do you listen to yourself? Have you looked around the world we live in? The lives we have?" Finally, I face her, but she doesn't look away. Her gaze so much like Zoltan's stays steady on mine. "We have hunters trying to kill us on a daily basis. Roberti doing his damn best to unleash Titans on all of us, traitors plotting our demise. And you ask me if it'd be so bad?"

She holds my gaze without saying a word for a long moment, while I do my best to control my breathing and stop my heart from punching a hole in my ribs. Tenebris wiggles closer, but not even the heat of his body can warm the ice curdling the blood in my veins. My brother's body chained to the metal bed pops in my head, which brings back the dread I felt finding him like that in Roberti's compound before I killed him with my own hand.

"Roberti is experimenting on half-bloods, Astara. Can you even imagine what would happen if he got his hands on an offspring from me and Zoltan?"

The words are not fully out of my mouth before both of us bolt upright, startling the shifter. He hisses angrily, but we ignore him.

"Oh, dear Fates." All the blood drains from my head, which makes me dizzy.

"You think he knew? That's why he started experimenting?" Astara looks like she's about to puke.

"It's too much of a coincidence if he started after I found out about his betrayal." Another thought comes to mind and it makes me seethe with rage. "He might've known it was possible before that, too. His lap dog Aiden, my partner, was pissed that I wasn't interested in jumping his bones while we were working together. Roberti even encouraged it with inconspicuous comments here and there."

"That's why the hunters are doing their best to hurt you but not kill you." When my eyebrows crawl up my forehead, she waves me off, jumps to her feet, and pulls me up. "If you saw it from my side, you'd know it was true. They only go for the kill when they see they're about to die. We must tell the others."

"We don't know if we are right." I'm running after her when she darts towards the academy, Tenebris looping next to me.

"But what if we are, Franky?" Her words come out in a rush. "What if we are?"

"Fuck. Here comes another clusterfuck."

Chapter Fourteen

Astara is nothing if not well organized. Plus, I believe most of the people in the building are scared of her, because the moment she enters the front doors like a whirlwind, everyone around jumps to do what she asked. In no time at all I find myself fidgeting, shuffling my feet, and staring at my toes in our makeshift war room, doing my best to ignore Zoltan's gaze.

I feel ridiculous for running out on him or blaming him for anything about my situation. The fact that I felt over-whelmed and needed to cry it out does not give me the right to shun him. But at that moment, I needed someone to blame—a person I could focus my anger and helplessness on so I didn't explode. In hindsight, I'm too embarrassed to look at him now, while guilt comes off him in waves.

So I mope, finding my dirty feet fascinating.

"I couldn't move Daren," Leo says on a sigh, closing the door behind him. "He is still recovering. That was a tough one on his magic."

"We can fill him in later." Astara is vibrating from the

need to tell them what we think is happening in the human realm.

I'm still hoping we are wrong.

Avoiding the intensity of Zoltan's eyes on me, I focus on Argoz, who I don't notice until now. For a change, the collar of his shirt looks as it should, not gaping down his chest because he's been tugging on it like crazy. Instead he is hugging something to his chest like his life depends on it, standing to the side away from all of us. When he notices me watching, I lift an eyebrow in question.

"The book is not safe if it's out of our sight." His arms tighten across his chest, muscles bulging from the effort. "They'll have to pry it from my dead arms if they want to take it again."

"You walk around with that damn thing in your hands?" Nothing could hide the incredulity in my voice. "Are you nuts?"

"Ghouls are known to be in prime form for four to five days with no sleep or food, Ms. Drake." He informs me formally as if he's holding a lecture. "At which point I will have my nephew take over so I can rest before resuming my duty. He is here at the academy and I vouch for his loyalty."

Soren ends up sitting next to me after switching a few chairs, as if the next one will be different under his royal ass or something. They are all wooden and uncomfortable, but what do I know about how it feels to him. His biceps strain while he struggles to tie his long hair, strands escaping his fingers enough times to piss me off. Huffing, I swat his hands away and gather his hair in mine, tying it at the back of his neck.

He even hands me an elastic band he must've snatched from someone at some point.

Fenrir will be my guess.

"And who will vouch for you, Argoz." I blurt out without thinking.

Leo and Zoltan groan at the same time.

Astara slaps a hand across her forehead.

I'm just confused.

"What-but-but ..." Argoz stutters, his face reddening to alarming levels. "I assure you I have been loyal to Sienna my entire life."

This time I groan as well.

Great. I insulted him.

"Sorry, I didn't mean it that way." My apology goes unheard.

"My father was—"

"We know, Argoz," Zoltan cuts him off, and that shuts the ghoul's mouth. "Francesca did not mean to question your loyalty. We all just want to make sure the book stays here and out of Roberti's hands."

I regret giving Zoltan a grateful look. He is not looking at Argoz at all, his full attention focused on my hands in Soren's hair. Soren, who is grinning like a fool at the vampire to get him to react.

I smack the back of the Fae's head and yank on his hair.

You can hear a pin drop.

"You really are an asshole." Ignoring everyone, I drop in my chair. "Would you stop provoking him for a second? We have stuff that's more important than you pissing Zoltan off."

It doesn't wipe the satisfied smile off his face, but I give him credit. He tries—and miserably fails—to look chastened. Damn Fae and their tricks. Like mischievous younglings, all they want is to cause trouble. And to prove my point, Zoltan walks behind my chair placing a possessive hand over my shoulder. Hiding my face in my hands, I'm debating if I should laugh or scream.

"Go ahead, Astara." Voice muffled through my hands, I sigh. "Tell them."

The longer she talks the thicker the tension is in the room. Leo keeps stealing glances my way, his gaze flicking between my face and my stomach. I squirm on the chair, uncomfortable with this whole bloodline continuation. Not that I can hold it against the alpha. Shifters are notorious when it comes to protecting their family, especially the younglings. I couldn't go anywhere without one of them popping out of the shadows. If what Soren claims is true, I dread the day I get pregnant.

Pregnant.

The word sends a mixture of emotions battering through me, and I realize I'm panting for breath when Zoltan tightens his hold on my shoulder in comfort. That's when Astara gets to our fear of why Roberti came up with the idea of creating his creatures. Even Soren looks disturbed by that thought, which is saying a lot. The insufferable male can't be fazed with anything unless it personally involves him.

"To what end?" Leo is clutching the back of the chair in a white-knuckled grip. "He was hell bent on releasing a Titan in the hopes that it will help him destroy the portals, and us with it. Why does he need half-bloods apart from the obvious? Humans are much easier to manipulate to become hunters than playing a god and mixing species. It doesn't make sense."

"I actually have a theory about that, too." Astara pushes off her chair and starts pacing.

Now that I see her properly in the light of the flames, I can tell she is much better. Her hair moves around her shoulders with each step and some color has returned to her face. The circles are still lingering like smudges under her eyes, but I'm no longer scared that she will drop on the ground at any second. Her clothing is loose on her frame, the fabric that normally hugs her curves bunching up in too many places for me not to notice.

"Franky is defying any facts we've gathered about half bloods." Giving me an apologetic look, she lifts her gaze to her brother standing behind my chair. "When you allowed him to take you, I'm pretty sure he took enough blood for his little projects. We were all aware that hurting you or luring Franky to come get you out was not all there was to it."

Tenebris apparently is done with lurking around, so he butts Soren's chair away from mine and squeezes his large body between us. Soren doesn't bat an eye, his entire focus on Astara. Grateful I don't have to argue with the ancient Fae, I glide my hand over the panther's head as he sits next to my legs and presses a giant paw over my foot.

"You think he is trying to create a creature from our mixed blood?" I feel lightheaded just thinking about it. "Why? What will he gain? All his creations that we've seen are like zombies for fuck's sake. He is playing Frankenstein."

"Who?" Soren sounds way too interested in the name, which makes my stomach churn fast enough that I'm scared I'll empty its contents all over the place.

"Never mind, it's a human thing." He doesn't look like he believes me, but I ignore him.

"Fenrir said Myst has a human associate that will help us destroy all the compounds we have a record of."

"We should keep that female away from here," Argoz murmurs, speaking for the first time since his lecture about the book. The mention of Myst has him wide eyed, and I'm surprised he isn't crossing himself and spitting over his shoulder. Not that I blame him. The female is really unhinged. Good thing she's on our side.

I snicker, which earns me a scowl from the ghoul.

"I think he is trying to create something resembling a youngling from the two of you without you actually breeding." No amount of apologies or sad looks can save Astara from my anger.

"I will kill them all if something like that has happened." Nostrils flaring, I can't keep myself from growling at her or from baring my fangs. "I'll destroy the human world along with him if what you say is true."

"Calm down, young dragon. That's your Dragon Blood talking and not you." Soren reaches for me but snatches his hand back when I hiss at him.

Throwing caution to the wind and hoping I won't hyperventilate again, I ask them what I didn't when we spoke in Zoltan's room. "Did you see him the same way I did through the portal?"

"Roberti?" Leo frowns, clenching his jaw. "I had to take Daren to the infirmary, so I didn't see any of it."

"What did you see?" Soren twists in his chair so he can face me.

"You didn't see Roberti staring at us?" Needing to hear them say it, I repeat myself.

"No," Soren answers simply and without inflection.

Craning my neck, I look behind me at Zoltan, but he only shakes his head. "But you talked to me when I saw him. You said he would have to go through you to hurt me."

"That is true, although I thought you were reflecting on the battle. I only saw the closed portal." Tucking loose hair behind my ear, he cups my face in his large palm. "What did you see, love? Is that why you panicked earlier? Talk to me, Francesca."

"Roberti was standing across the portal." Swallowing the bile and terror, I keep my gaze on his to stay grounded. "The shadows that were killing through Sienna were attached to him. Like him and them were one and the same. They were wreathing and bellowing behind him like a sentient cloak." Through numb lips, I pushed the last part out. "He saw me, too, Zoltan."

"Fascinating." We all look at Soren like he's lost his mind. "Females of my kind are known to have many special powers others do not. They guarded them with their lives, and I thought it was just a myth." His glowing lock on mine. "You are a rare gem indeed, young dragon."

"Keep your creepy self away from me, dumbass, or I swear I'll fry your ass." Blurting the first thing that comes to mind, I scoot the chair away from him. "You've been awake for too long. I think you're going coocoo. Go get some rest."

"I've slept for a long time." Narrowing his gaze, he smiles eerily at me. "Maybe a little too long."

"Zoltan?" Jerking my eyes away from the old fart, I stare at the vampire while stabbing a finger at Soren's face. "Here is your chance to shine. Do your caveman shit. Beat him with a club across the head if you want to because I'm seriously freaked out right now."

Astara busts out laughing, but I find nothing funny about this.

"You believe me bad?" Soren snickers, and I don't like what I see in his eyes. "Did you ask your mate why he is called the Blood King?"

I do remember asking Zoltan but he kinda dodged my question and I left it at that. Too many things happening at once makes me forget the little things. The important one obviously, at least if I'm judging by how excited the Fae is.

"That's not who he is now." Astara jumps to her brother's defense, but I keep my gaze glued on Zoltan.

"You truly are trouble, Soren," Leo mumbles on a sigh.

"Before the Purge I was not the same male." Tilting his chin up, the vampire stares me down as if daring me to judge him. "Times were different; it was every male to his own. Only the strongest survived, so I made sure I was stronger than all of them. I drank the blood of those standing in my way to the last drop and left their bodies for everyone to see, which earned me the name Blood King. I am the oldest living vampire, so king is a title that came from my bloodline, not by my actions."

A shiver runs down my spine. Then I see a flicker of something in Zoltan's gaze that snaps me out of the stupid thoughts trying to make me fear him or look at him differently. Whoever he was centuries ago is not the Zoltan I know now. The one ready to sacrifice himself to protect others. No wonder he gave up his true form in his oath. Even now I can see the guilt eating at him inside. Others may not notice, but I've watched him when he has his guard down enough to know the male better than anyone.

"Where do you think we should leave Soren's body after we drain him dry?" Zoltan's eyes widen comically at my comment. "And then you'll have to share Blood King. Plus, the more Soren talks, the better the idea sounds, don't you think?"

"The Fates always choose well." Soren shakes his head chuckling.

"We can entertain you later, Soren," Astara snaps at him, still angry for his assholish behavior. "What are we doing about Roberti?"

"Can the three of you leave through the portal and fight?" Even Leo perks at my question, his typical grin bringing back a small part of the friend I'm used to seeing.

"I'm not sure, but I'm willing to try," Astara says too eagerly.

"If we can remove all the excess magic coursing through us, it might help us gain control too." Rolling his shoulders, Leo looks at Soren for confirmation.

"I do not see the harm in that." Unfolding gracefully from the chair, he looks down at me. "What do you have in mind, young dragon?"

"A field trip." My grin stretches my lips. "I hope you can glamour humans to not be able see us. I'm not wearing another pink shirt with a glittering unicorn."

Leo's laughter is music to my ears.

Chapter Fifteen

"You really don't need to bring all those weapons." Arms folded over my chest, I lean on the closed door watching Zoltan move around the weapon's room.

The black shirt stretches tight across his shoulders and back giving me the perfect view of every muscle bunching as he picks up swords, crossbow, and daggers, stashing them in the many pockets of his pants. The crossbow gets hooked on his belt, hanging down almost to his knee. Now that I've seen him walk the daylight, I can't help but admire the edge given to him by the bright silver moonlight and flickering orange glow of the dancing flames. They form shadows on his handsome features, making his cheekbones look sharper and his square jaw more defined.

It still bothers me that he knew things about our bond and kept them from me, but looking at the bigger picture, I can't say I blame him. I do have a penchant to react first then think later. Would it have mattered if he said something? I'm not sure, and with everything still tense and fucked up, I realize I don't even care at this point. Rubbing my fist between my breasts hoping to elevate the pressure I feel there, I see him turn to look at me over his shoulder, a line forming between his brows when he notices what I'm doing.

"I don't need them, but they might come in handy."

Tucking one last dagger on his thigh, he prowls closer to me, each step measured and with purpose. My heartbeat picks up from the intensity in his blue gaze, which glides over my body from head to toes and back. Mouth drying up the closer he gets, my tongue pokes out to wet my perched lips.

It doesn't go unnoticed.

The right corner of his mouth twitches slightly and his eyes narrow at the pulse in my neck.

"If I didn't know better, I'd say you were nervous, love."

I shiver from the raspy tone of his deep voice, pressing my back to the unforgiving door behind me as if that will help me not to feel the heat of his body when he stops an inch from my toes. The arrogant smirk grows the longer my eyes stay glued to his lips until I forcefully jerk them up to his face.

"Keep dreaming, jackass." Pretending I didn't hear the squeak in my voice, I jut my chin out stubbornly. "Being pissed off and being nervous are two different things."

"This"—Lifting his hand, he feathers the tip of his finger down the column of my throat—"tells me otherwise."

"We are going to war." Unwilling to admit that he still controls the reactions of my body more than I do, I scoff at him. "What do you want me to do? Dance the Macarena?"

"The what now?" Tucking his chin, Zoltan searches my face like he is judging my sanity.

It's easy to forget how old he is by the way he talks and acts most of the time.

"Nothing you would understand, old man." Grinning when he glowers, I try to slide away from him but his hand slaps the door next to my head stopping my escape.

"I don't remember you saying I'm an old male last night." Nudging the tip of his nose on mine, Zoltan's lips graze mine and I choke on the moan that tries to escape.

"You are so humble it's mindboggling." My attempt to shove him away is useless. It only presses me closer to his chest, and he pins me to the door and slides his thigh between my legs.

"Tell me, Francesca." My name rolls off his tongue in a purr that pebbles my skin. "Would you have given me a second glance if I was humble?"

Ducking his head, he glides his lips and tongue up my neck, stopping at my ear before nipping on it. There is no way he didn't feel my body shudder against his. His low chuckle confirms my fear and heat pools in my lower belly.

"You don't need humble, love." Hot breath puffs the back of my ear and I close my eyes. "What you need is someone to take control while you fight him tooth and nail for it."

My eyes snap open so I can glare at him. "Get off me."

When he moves a step away to give me space it's like a slap across my face, but I swallow my disappointment even though it's not easy. My lips press in a thin line as I try to sidestep him so I'm not cornered, hoping the heat crawling up my neck is not noticeable to him. Tough chance that, but a girl can dream. The fact that his words hit too close to home is another matter I'm adamant to ignore.

If I wasn't avoiding his gaze, I would've seen him move.

One second I'm looking at the soft mats of the room, and the next second said room spins fast as my arm is yanked behind my back and I find my face pushed to the door with Zoltan's weight on me. Short breaths laden with anticipation waft across the side of my face when he leans his chest harder on me.

"Are you trying to run, love?" There is no mistaking the predatory tone in his words. I fell for the oldest trick in the book.

A predator wanted to play, and I made the first move.

Heartbeat accelerating, wetness dampens my panties.

Zoltan takes a deep breath from behind me, a too-low growl vibrating his chest. "Tell me again how I'm wrong."

"Fuck you, Zoltan."

"That's the plan, love."

His hold tightens around my wrist and he pushes my arm closer to my back, while his other arm snakes around my waist tugging my ass against his groin. His hardness nestles between my ass cheeks weakening my knees. With barely-there contact, his hand slides underneath my shirt, his strong fingers splaying across my stomach. Out of my control, my back arches and rubs me against him.

"Stop fighting me on this, Francesca." The tips of his fangs graze the hollow where my neck meets my shoulder, and nothing can stop my husky moan.

Zoltan chuckles.

The tips of his fingers dip in the waistband of my pants, deftly unbuttoning the buttons one after another, each tug of the fabric driving me insane. Zoltan is toying with me, taking his time as a way of punishment because I'll never admit out loud how much I crave him. I was determined not to admit it anyway, but the second those same fingers push inside my panties and dive between my wet folds, I forget my own name and my stubbornness flies out the window.

"Look how much your body wants me," he purrs in my ear, his fingers gliding to circle my button. "It tells me everything those pretty lips refuse to say."

Reduced to a whimpering mess, I moan and grind against his fingers while trying to escape his hold on my other arm. Giving me a reprieve, he guides my arm to the side before pressing my palm on the door and covering it with his own hand. When I try to move it, he nips on my shoulder hard enough to sting, but not hard enough to break the skin.

"Keep it there, love."

My lips part to say something, but I can't even remember what when he yanks my pants and panties down to my knees. All I manage is a gasp before he is there, grinding his erection and the buttons of his own pants against me. I writhe and moan like a possessed female. His fingers never stop moving, infuriatingly missing the place where I need him most.

"Zoltan." Growling his name through clenched teeth, I chase his fingers, which elicits a chuckle from him.

"What do you need, love?" One thick finger slides inside me, but it's gone before I have a chance to enjoy it.

Pressing my lips together, I refuse to play this game with him. I guess I still have a bit of sanity left. If he wants to wait for me to say it, he'll be waiting a very long time. A second finger joins the first, and my eyes roll back in my head as I forget why I was upset or why it is such a bad idea to just tell him whatever he wants to hear. Luckily, only moans and gasps pass my lips.

Zoltan keeps torturing me for what feels like an eternity, turning me into a puddle of need. Inarticulate sounds are coming from my parted lips, and my quivering knees can barely hold my weight, yet he won't end my misery. Just when I'm about to start begging him for anything he is willing to give, I hear the rustle of fabric from behind me. That is enough to hurl me into an intense orgasm with bright lights blinding me from behind my closed eyelids. A satisfied male chuckle that would've pissed me off if I wasn't riding the high surrounds me from all sides. When the jerking and trembling stops, I sag in his hold while panting for breath.

"So stubborn." The amused drawl is my only warning.

Zoltan steps back, taking my lower body with him. The buckle of his belt thumps on the floor before both his hands wrap tightly around my hips and he enters me in one hard thrust.

I scream.

The entire building can probably hear me, but at the moment I couldn't care less. Zoltan releases the control on our bond, blasting me with the crippling hunger he was hiding, and I drown in it. There is nothing left of the arrogant tease from a moment ago. The bruising hold on my hips stays while he pounds in me for all he is worth, and I have no other choice but to press my hands on the door so I don't end up pummeled into it. Magic swirls in the center of my chest and colors start dancing around us when I open my eyes.

"Let go." Zoltan's voice sounds much deeper, a warning that he is releasing his true form even while his shaft swells inside me, the intensity bordering on a pleasure-pain.

I know he is asking me to release my own control, but I hesitate. I don't hold back because of fear for myself. At the moment I can barely think. I'm worried the magic might burst out of me again and bring the entire building down on our heads. Then the damn vampire changes his angle and all thoughts float away on a cloud of pleasure and need.

"Let go, love," he growls again, and I do.

Claws sprout from my fingertips and sink into the wooden door like butter, and my lips twist in a snarl that bares my fangs. Zoltan's cock pounds inside me, and the tightness of the coil in my stomach builds to unbearable levels. My moans turn into crazed hisses and snarls as I give as much as I get, pushing back toward him, the sound of our skin slapping together echoing through the wide room. Grunts and growls coming from Zoltan join them, his tempo getting faster until he lifts my body to hold it a few inches off the floor. It prevents me from moving, though it doesn't stop me from trying.

I arch and snake my back until my feet hit the ground with the intention of turning around. One of Zoltan's hands disappears for a second before it wraps my hair around his wrist, keeping me pinned in front of him. He yanks my upper body up, bringing his mouth to my neck. My heart jumps in excitement and pummels my ribcage in expectation of his bite. His second hand, which is on my hip, disappears too.

My blood turns to ice when I feel the slice of a dagger on my neck.

Jerking my head around, I see the glint of a golden dagger, the jewel-crusted hilt firmly held in Zoltan's hand. Panic wars with pleasure until my thoughts are muddied. My mouth opens and closes a few times, but I can't get a single word to come out.

"Soren's dagger for forming the bond." Zoltan grunts, but he somehow keeps the fast temp of his thrusts.

"How?" That's all I'm capable of saying.

I watch in fascination as he pulls out of me and turns me around to face him. Lifting the dagger, he makes the same cut on his own neck before dropping it on the ground. My greedy eyes rove over his muscled thighs and his bobbing erection, which is glistening with my juices. The shirt has ridden up and is sticking to his torso above his laser-cut abs. Blinking stupidly, I force myself to look at his face.

"I know you, Francesca." Lifting a hand, he moves the hair sticking to my sweaty forehead. "Soren would've wanted to witness the bond and that is not what you want. Things that are private to you are things you want to keep close to your heart. Not for all to see." A sheepish smile tilts his lips. "He was so occupied with making preparations for the human realm that it was too easy to swipe it without him noticing."

My gaze drops to the rivulet of blood trickling from the cut down his neck. He growls but doesn't move, waiting to see my reaction to this. Warmth spreads through my entire being when he bares his neck in offering. Soren made a decision for me when I was born that I had no say in, and so did my father right alongside Fenrir. No matter how well-meaning their intentions were, those choices weren't mine.

Zoltan is giving me a real choice, and I can feel how much it costs him to hold back in this moment.

Scrambling fast, I struggle out of my boots and pants, kicking them to the side. My hand reaches for him, and the next thing I know my back hits the door and my legs are wrapped around his narrow hips. One large hand grabs a hold of my ass, and he lifts me as he sinks inside me. It's a perfect fit, like my body was made just for him. Shifting to look at my face, he delivers the biggest shock of my life.

"I love you, my mate." Tears prickle my eyes. "Your

blood is my blood. Your body is my body. Your death is my death. From this day until our souls are no more."

Like I'm in a daze, I feel my lips moving and my voice repeats the same words to him. His fangs sink into the cut in my neck and mine follow suit. Zoltan keeps thrusting, this time his movements slower, more leisured, building the tension in me back to the same level as before. Potent, powerful blood fills my mouth and slides down my throat until my body ignites into a raging inferno.

I'm burning.

My body feels like I will disintegrate to ashes, yet everywhere we touch our skin is as cold as ice. My back bows when Zoltan increases his speed, holding one hand under my ass to protect me from hitting the door. The coil tightens inside me and I bite into his neck harder, which has him snarling even as he does the same. On his last thrust, his pelvic bone slams mine from the strength hurling me into an oblivion. Ripping my mouth away from his neck, I let out a scream that's not actually a scream or my voice, though it rattles the walls in this room.

A roar with ancient power rains plaster around us.

When Zoltan joins me in orgasm, one more thrust hits me hard, and it has dark spots dancing at the corners of my eyes. Despite that I force my eyes to stay open as I watch him, completely mesmerized. With his head thrown back and the muscles of his shoulders, arms, and neck straining, Zoltan is the most beautiful thing I have ever seen in my life. Gasping and sucking gulps of air, I can't help but grin when he looks at me and gives me a simple smile. The fire in my blood is still moving through my veins and goosebumps cover me from head to toe.

"Do you feel it, too? The heat?" Rasping through my raw throat, I try to slow my breathing.

"Yes." The smile turns into a smirk and I narrow my eyes on him.

"Why do I have a feeling there was some fine print I didn't read?"

"No, love." Chuckling, he shakes his head, a lock of dark hair falling over his forehead. "No fine print. I swear it on my life."

"What then?"

"I think we better get dressed." Lowering me gently on the ground, he holds onto me until I can lock my knees. "I have a feeling Soren heard that."

"Ah, fuck!" I elbow Zoltan because he laughs, though I can't stop my own snort when I think about the ancient Fae losing his shit for missing this.

Chapter Sixteen

"Why do I need to wear this ... this abomination?" Soren tilts his head back so he can glare at me through the football helmet I shoved on his head.

"Because it's been centuries since you've walked through the portal." Keeping a straight face has never been this difficult. "A decade ago they discovered it protects your powers, so if you are attacked when you exit on the other side, you won't be blindsided and powerless like a newborn babe."

The ancient Fae narrows his eyes on me, but he doesn't argue. He was all about me dressing him in a pink tutu with glitter, his dragon perking up about shiny things. In a million years, though, he never expected this. Neither did I if I'm being honest, but I thought of it the last second when he started raving about not being the one to seal the bond between Zoltan and me.

"I have never heard of such a thing." He scoffs, but he doesn't remove it. Fates forbid he doesn't have access to his powers.

Zoltan and Leo sound like they are coughing out a lung,

and both pound on their chests to cover their laughter. Even Daren, as pale as he is while leaning heavily on Astara, snorts, chokes, and ducks his head. Zoltan's sister is my only ally, and her serious expression and confident nod supports my claims.

Turning to the portal, tremors whisper up and down my spine until goosebumps pop up all over my skin like some kind of premonition. Shoving it down, I square my shoulders because I'm unwilling to show everyone gathered here that I'm still dreading nearing the swirling magic, that I'm imagining all sorts of crazy scenarios playing out the second we get near it.

Tenebris rubs his head on my hip- what's a gentle nudge to the shifter, is a hard shove for me,- pushing me to stumble to the side. Snickering nervously, I place my hand between his shoulder blades, comforted by his presence. Zoltan moves closer, too, the heat of his body warming my back and adding more reassurance. I'm not sure what I'm expecting to happen, but whatever it is, there is a feeling in my gut that it'll be the mother of all clusterfucks. Remembering the shadow writhing around my old boss like a menace brings acid roof of my mouth, and it burns.

"Did anyone let Fenrir and Myst know that we are going?" Keeping my voice low so only those close to me can hear, I look from one person to the other.

"I sent word." Leo frowns as he rubs his jaw. "I didn't hear anything back. They know where we are headed, so I'm sure if they can get away, they'll meet us there. The two of you were otherwise occupied when I was coming to tell you." His mouth kicks up to the side in a cocky grin, but it doesn't reach his eyes. "I didn't want Zoltan to feel inadequate, so I didn't join the party."

My hand shoots out snatching Zoltan back when he

snarls and surges toward the alpha. Leo dances back a few steps while chortling with both arms lifted to the sides with his palms up. Shaking my head at his silliness, I laugh myself. Leo being Leo has managed to lighten my mood, even if his own laughter is a bit forced. Pulling my eyes away from him, I look behind us.

Around fifty of the most skillful fighters wait impatiently a couple of yards away talking quietly among each other. When any of them make eye contact with me, their fist thumps the center of their chest and they offer a slight nod. One I return while making sure my fear for their lives doesn't show on my face.

"They know we have no idea what we are up against apart from that asshole Andrius, right?" The question is a murmur to Zoltan, who is staring daggers at Leo. I jab him in the ribs to get his attention. "Yes?"

"They know, love." Wrapping a possessive arm across my chest, he tugs me to him while keeping his slanted gaze on the alpha. Leo's grin grows and he wiggles his eyebrows. "All of them volunteered to join the mission." The last word ends in a growl and I shake my head again.

"Hold on to that anger, and when we go across, unleash your cute ass on the hunters. Deal?" Zoltan's head snaps in my direction so fast that I have no idea how he doesn't break his neck. "What?"

"You think my ass is cute?" The way a smile slowly blooms on his scowling face is art in the making.

I glare at him.

"Seriously? That's all you got from what I just said?" Scoffing, I shrug him off, but it doesn't wipe off the stupid grin.

Cracking my neck, I inch closer to Tenebris. Like the amazing creature that he is, he slinks between us and hisses at Zoltan. Amusement blasts me through our bond that apparently stays wide open now, and that means I can't hide shit from the Daywalker. Of course he is ecstatic about that fact. Though that is probably the main reason he is on edge, too. He feels my trepidation and anxiety about facing Roberti. Not, per se, about the demigod himself. I have enough anger to beat him to a pulp if the chance presents itself. It's more about whatever poisons and monstrosities he has created while we were busy playing defense. He has kept us chasing our tail or looking over our shoulder so much we haven't had time to find him and end this once and for all.

That game of cat and mouse stops now.

"I shall remove this thing when I cross to the other side," Soren announces, as if that is the most important thing right now. Of course the Fae is more concerned with the damn helmet than the lives of those coming with us.

"If your brain is intact then you can remove it, yes," I tell him absentmindedly.

I may have laughed at the gasp that follows my words, but I'm wound up too tight for that.

Without too much fanfare, all of us head for the portal. The spinning of the colors intensifies. I see the guards standing to the sides watching us leave, all their faces solemn. The alert eyes of the shifters in their animal forms are also locked on us, and my heart is kicking like a wild horse against my ribs. I clench my hands so no one will see them trembling.

I'm the first to reach the portal, and Tenebris and I both step through it at the same time with Zoltan on our heels. The hard tug at the center of my chest as I'm propelled through the magic and spat out on the other side is barely noticeable now. Landing on my feet, my knees buckle but I hurriedly move to the side to make space for those coming behind me.

The three of us watch Leo pop up next, followed by Astara and Daren. The mage doesn't look worse than before he passed the portal, so it gives me some piece of mind. What frustrates me to no end, however, is Soren coming through surrounded by four other people with him in the center. The moment he steps through he yanks the helmet off, holding it away from him with a thumb and forefinger like it's a dirty diaper.

"My magic is intact," the ancient Fae informs us formally, as if all of us were worried about his stupid powers.

Astara gives me a quick glance, biting the inside of her lips to hide a smile.

"Perfect." Striding down the alley that is surprisingly missing the stench of urine and decay, I turn my back on him. "Keep it close for when we go back, just in case."

When I turn to peer at him over my shoulder, he frowns before tucking the helmet under his arm. Astara's soft giggle makes me smile as well. Soren might be an ass, but he is very entertaining.

We time the crossing to make sure it's nighttime in the human realm, figuring it'll be easier for Soren to wave his illusion and hide us from prying eyes, which is something we shouldn't have worried about judging by the magic washing over me like a soft summer breeze as if whispering over my skin. All of us move in a progression of two or three people, making it possible to pass the few humans still lingering on the streets.

Horns blare and sirens wail in the distance, and Soren jerks his head left and right to search for whatever is making the noise. I guess I looked the same the first time I came here, although I'd like to think I did it less obviously. The hoots and shouts reach my ears before I see them.

From around the corner, a half a dozen or so humans dressed in dark clothing with chains hanging from their belts and the smell of gunpower on their skin come right at us. The couple in the front swagger with more confidence than Soren in front of the old Order of the academy. It says a lot since the damn Fae is still not wearing a shirt.

The humans spread out, their eyes darting around to look for the threat they can feel but can't see. I watch Zoltan from the corner of my eye slide to my right, and surprisingly Daren straightens, pushing off of Astara. Tenebris glides away from me to circle them from the side when the humans stop, their hands going to whatever weapons they carry.

"They can't see us," Zoltan says under his breath, just loud enough for me to hear him. "When you live a life like theirs, you sense danger before it finds you. It's what keeps them alive." I could be wrong, but I think I hear him mumble *until now*.

Magic spits and crackles from Daren's fingertips, while the mage shakes his hands like he is trying to loosen his stiff muscles. My own body angles itself in preparation of an attack, but then understanding hits me like an anvil across the head. The damn initiation is going to force us all to remove the threat to us and the humans. I wish I realized faster how wrong I was. It has nothing to do with the initiation.

The fighters that followed us here stand to the side with confusion twisting their features.

"Leo, can't you stop this shit?" My voice rings out louder than I intended, and a gun goes off, the bullet whizzing a hairsbreadth away from my face.

Zoltan snarls and turns into a killing machine.

My jaw drops as I watch him move graceful as a dancer, twisting and turning, his arms and legs executing perfect kicks and punches without missing a target. From one breath to the next, he stands in the middle of a pile of bodies, their necks in unnatural angles and their eyes open as they stare unseeing in different directions. Baring his fangs, the vampire snarls again, his enraged gaze searching for more people to kill. Soren snickers from behind me, and that earns him a scowl.

"How very interesting." The Fae's calculating stare moves from Zoltan, to me, and back.

"Whatever." Ignoring his dumb ass, I look expectantly at Leo. "This shit is getting old. Can't the three of you remove the urge to remove any threat to humanity? Or, I don't know, maybe you can switch it to something else. Awe don't have time to fight the humans now." Flicking my wrist around, I lift both eyebrows in question. "Plus, it can be used against us if Roberti knows about it. And with that jerk Casius in his pocket, trust me, he knows."

"I haven't thought of it." The alpha exchanges looks with Astara and Daren but both of them shrug.

My mouth opens to tell them to start thinking fast, but more hoots and screams come from across the four-lane road. I flinch when something slams into glass and shatters it like a waterfall of tinkling sounds. For the first time since we walked out of the alley that protects our portal, I look around the human city.

Really look.

The bright colors from the storefronts I grew accustomed to seeing are dimmed and boards are placed over most of the doors. The glare of the streetlights casts shadows across the street where cars drive faster than usual, the humans operating the vehicles clutching the steering wheels in a death grip. Releasing my magic just enough to shift my perception, I lift my face and sniff the air.

The cloying odors of terror and rage burn my nostrils, and the breath I take is like a punch to the gut making me stumble back. Frantic, I turn to Zoltan only to find him clawing at the bodies at his feet since there is no one else around him to kill. Astara's fangs are out as well, her gaze burning with hunger and locked on her brother. Daren is turning into a firework's show, and Leo's face starts contouring to announce he's about to shift.

"Soren?" Inching closer to the Fae, I don't take my eyes off them. Even the people that came with us start shifting, and the ones without a second form are becoming more aggressive. "What the fuck is happening?"

"I do not know, young dragon, but it does not feel right." A line puckering his brows is the only sign of his distress, but I feel it.

Zoltan's fury is scratching the insides of my ribs through our bond, becoming more difficult to ignore. My connection to Soren is brimming with worry unlike anything I've felt from the old Dragon Blood before. That more than anything else freaks me out, and I have to fight to stay in my right mind. Ancient old magic is trying to take control over my actions, the horrid whispers coming with it chilling my blood.

This is bad.

Really bad.

"Can you stop it?" Pushing the words through clenched teeth, I eye Tenebris, who is becoming more agitated. "Like now would be the perfect time, Soren."

"I can create a shield clearing the air around some of

them, but not all." The Fae is still watching everything as if it doesn't faze him.

"Do it!" Shoving him in front of me, I stab a finger at Zoltan and my friends. "Shield them. They are most dangerous. I can deal with the others in the meantime. I'll just knock their asses out."

Just as Soren starts murmuring in a lyrical language I don't understand, a large SUV screeches around the corner, the back of it fishtailing before it jerks to a stop in front of me. The driver door swings open and Myst jumps out of it, her grin so wide it's scarier than Zoltan when he is pissed off.

"Hey Chicca, nice company you've got there." Swinging her hips, her metal six-inch heels click on the pavement when she comes around. "Get their asses in the car and get out of here. It's not as bad in the outskirts of the city, so they'll be fine."

"Where is Fenrir?" There is something different about her, but I can't put my finger on it.

"He'll be here in no time, so don't worry your pretty head." Giggling, she ignores Soren like he doesn't exist. "Last time I escaped him, he caught up in three minutes on foot. I was in my car." Shrugging and shaking her head like she can't believe he even dared, she points at the car again. "Go, it'll only get worse and I can't linger long either. Eventually it'll get to me too, and no one wants this crazy girl to lose it. Trust me." Shuddering, she removes the thumb she was pointing at herself with.

"Soren, help me put them in the car."

Myst and her crazy behavior can wait until later. If she's saying it's bad, that means shit has hit the fan. I watch the Fae push the five of them toward the SUV and they listen only because they look dazed.

"What's going on, Myst?" Watching her for any indication that she's brushing me off, my heart stops when all humor leaves her face.

"I have no idea, but it started yesterday. The oppressive feeling dropped over the city like a fog out of nowhere. The humans are losing their shit."

"What about them?" Pointing at the people we brought with us, I cringe when I find them fighting each other. What a fucking mess.

"I got them. You drive outside the city and I'll meet you there." Shoving me towards the car, she moves to the center of the sidewalk. "Shoo, go!"

Holding the door open after I take her place in the driver's seat, I wait to see what she is going to do.

Fenrir comes running from the same corner the SUV arrived from, his face scrunched in anger. Myst laughs happily before placing two fingers on her lips, and a piercing whistle stops the fight. Every eye turns her way and she grins.

"This way ladies and gentleman." Slapping a hand on her hip, she scratches her arm and a horse-sized hellhound materializes out of nowhere, a long thick chain leashing him to her wrist. "If you assholes want to fight, how about picking on someone your size," said the female who is five feet two inches without her heels.

Spinning on her heels, she bolts down the street, her hound ahead of her. Everyone darts after her as if she's a willing prey.

"What in all the fucks was that?" I ask no one in particular as I slam the door closed.

"The Fates giving me another slap across the face," Soren answers glumly just as I gun it, following Myst, too.

Chapter Seventeen

Taking turns left and right to avoid all the drivers that want to play chicken, who are heading right at me instead of keeping to their own lane, I clutch the steering wheel so hard it starts groaning. Eyes darting left and right, I'm doing my best to stay focused on reaching the outskirts of the city, but the nagging feeling in my gut makes it difficult to concentrate. The frosty bite in the air when we crossed the portal was very subtle, and I didn't think anything of it until we came across the group of hostile humans. None of the others made a comment about it either. Zoltan, who is cunningly alert and observant when it comes to things like this, being quiet left us all open for whatever stupidity this turns out to be.

"Is everyone good back there?" Keeping my eyes on the road, my voice echoes in the silent car.

"They can't hear you," Soren chirps absentmindedly from the passenger seat. "I made the protection thick enough to hold the clean air inside and not let anything in from the outside." Twisting around, he leans back to check on them. "They all look well, although ... I believe Zoltan is unhappy."

In other words, the vampire is pissed as all hell and ready to bite heads off. Soren, I've noticed, likes to downplay situations however it suits him. With a noncommittal hum, I yank on the steering wheel to avoid a pothole on the road as deep as a crater. Deep down I know Roberti has something to do with this, but the problem is I can't tell what. Did he release a poison to make all the humans go nuts? That's definitely something he is capable of. Especially if it'll further his plans.

"Your magic is changing." I see Soren wrinkling his nose as he shifts uncomfortably in his seat.

There is a painful thump against my ribs.

"Changing how?" Keeping my voice level to keep him talking, I clear my throat. "Whatever is going on didn't affect me like it did the rest. I felt the chill and the difference in the air, but I mostly reacted from Zoltan's rage through the bond." Giving him a side glance, I figure I better just get everything out while I'm at it. "And your worry and confusion came out loud and clear ... through the blood bond."

My body jerks forward when the four in the backseat shuffle, but I tighten my hold and don't look in the rearview mirror. Last time my eyes darted there, Zoltan's blue gaze locked on me burning with anger. I know it's not aimed at me because I feel it through our bond, but if you've never looked into the face of a furious vampire, you'll never understand how unsettling it is. It brings all your survival instincts to the forefront of your mind and you can't think. All you want to do is run.

"I am not sure." Soren's elegant fingers caress the top of

the helmet sitting in his lap, which he hasn't let out of his sight. "It's not from the magic in the air." Twirling his wrist, he indicates the outside through his window.

"So it's not a poison." Slumping in the seat, air gushes out of me in a whoosh, deflating my lungs. "Okay, good. This is good. Magic I can work with."

"Poison?" Soren snorts like that's the stupidest thing he has ever heard. "That out there, young dragon, is much, much worse."

"You know what it is?"

I look at him sharply but have to turn away when sirens blare and I almost crash into a pickup truck. The back of the SUV fishtails as I jerk the steering wheel left and right, tapping my foot to press and release the breaks without flipping us over. Cold sweat drenches the back of my shirt as I remember the last time I was in this same car flipping over with hunters dead set on killing us.

"Control this contraption," Soren snaps.

It takes me long moments but all four tires finally hit the road with a bouncy jump, and I straighten the car to move it the way it should move. When I look at Soren, I wish I wasn't stressed so much, otherwise I'd laugh in his face. Arms outstretched, he has one hand gripping the door handle hard enough to bend the plastic. The other hand is pressed to the dashboard, and the damn helmet is shoved over his left knee, which he holds up so he does not to lose the protection of his powers. Face blanched and golden eyes too wide, it looks like he is trying to keep the car from collapsing in on itself.

"Welcome to the twenty first century in the human world, old fart."

Mocking him, I bark out a hysterical laugh and slow when I come to an intersection. Familiar buildings come into view, and for some reason I take a sharp left, gunning the car in the direction of the forest shielding the other portal.

It feels as if we should be there.

As we near the woods, I can already feel the lessening of whatever magic surrounds the city. Clenching my jaw, I don't mention it to Soren in case he decides to release the protection and I have to listen to Zoltan yelling. He might not be angry at me, but he won't be too pleased to be kept in a bubble. Literally.

When we reach as far as we can get in a vehicle, I hit the brakes and stare ahead without saying a word. My hands feel glued to the steering wheel and I force my fingers open one by one. Uncomfortable tingles spread through my palms and up my arms like they've been numb for hours. Puffing my cheeks, I blow out a breath and finally turn in my seat to face the Fae.

"Release the protection." When he doesn't move, I keep him pinned under my gaze. "Release them and you can get out of the car if you want."

The door is open and he is jumping outside before I'm done talking. The helmet drops to the ground, but he spins mid-jump and scoops it up as graceful as a ballerina, bouncing on his toes a couple of times before he straightens. The frosty glare he sends my way doesn't have the affect he expects when the four people in the car start talking at the same time. Out of everything I hear, one thing is like a nail to my head.

"Francesca, we will have words about this," Zoltan growls from the back seat.

"Really?" Twisting around to look at him, I give the vampire a cloyingly sweet smile. "No 'thank you, Franky? You stopped us from making assess of ourselves.' Or, better yet, 'thank you, Francesca.'" Mimicking his deep voice, I scowl at him. "That was fast thinking and now that we have control of our minds we can fix this shit. No? Nothing? Oh well, I did try!"

Jumping out of the car, I slam the door hard enough to dent it and stop on the other side where Soren is still keeping a narrowed gaze on me. Tough crowd, this bunch. No matter what you do, they're never happy. Before I reach the Fae, my feet leave the ground and I'm flipped around to face Zoltan, my boots hanging a foot of the floor.

"What were you thinking?" the vampire roars at my face, shaking me hard enough to rattle my teeth.

My foot swings and I nail him his in his family jewels. He drops me when he doubles over. My body keeps reacting on its own no matter what I do. Next, my knee connects with his face and throws him on his back. Blood spills down his mouth and chin, and I gasp as I take a step back.

"This is your fault." Stabbing a finger at his bloodied, pissed-off face is not very smart because my hand is trembling, and that only kills my badass vibe. "I have kneejerk reactions when I'm startled, which is a fact you know all too well."

At least Soren finds it funny because he's giggling like a little girl behind me.

"It wasn't Drake's doing," Leo says to no one in particular, leaning a shoulder on the back door of the SUV. "It felt like it was coming from her, but that back there was not her power."

"What are you talking about?" Confused, I glance at the alpha but keep Zoltan in view at all times. The jerk is about jump me and take me home to lock me up. I can feel it.

"I thought it was either Franky or Soren, as well." Daren watches me with both brows lowered over his eyes.

Dark smudges under them make the green of his irises stand out as if his eyes are glowing. "It felt old ... ancient."

"Wait a second?" Slapping both hands on my hips, I glare at them. "You thought I did that? Why in the worlds would I do something so stupid?"

"The stench of it was like nothing I've smelled before." Leo's face twists in a grimace. Shuddering, he rubs a hand up and down his pebbled arm. "Decay smells like roses compared to that."

"The seals have been broken.," Soren tells us with a thoughtful look plastered all over his face. "The question is, how. And are they open or merely just cracked enough to let magic seep into this world."

"The seals of what?" I know the answer because its squeezing my lungs like a fist, but I have to ask.

Zoltan lifts on an elbow and starts getting up, so I shuffle away from him and step closer to Tenebris. At least the panther hasn't accused me of trying to turn everyone into killers. It could be because he can't talk, but I don't care.

"The deepest pits of the underworld." The tone of Soren's voice makes it seem like he is telling us the grass is a nice shade of green.

Numbness makes the back of my skull tingle.

"The Titans." Silence falls over us like a heavy blanket pressing onto our shoulders. I can't feel the words passing my lips. "How? We got the book back." Remembering the redhead and how much she hated me, I wouldn't put it past her to trick me just as a fuck you from her grave. "Did anyone check if the book was intact?"

"Intact?" Astara frowns, her lips mushed together in a thin, white line.

"The pages. Did it have all the pages?" Every set of eyes turn on me like I just sprouted a second head. "She had half of her body on our side of the portal, and that was the half holding the book. If that was me, I'd switch hands so it made it to where it was intended to go. Especially if I was going to die anyway."

"That's easy to check." Leo looks over my shoulder at the forest hiding the portal from view. "I can be there and back in thirty minutes tops."

"Go," Daren encourages the alpha, his gaze moving over the trees as if searching for something. "We should know what we are up against before rushing blindly into this."

"We will wait here." Zoltan makes a decision for all of us as he swipes the back of his hand under his nose, smudging the blood across his cheek. "The city is not safe if we can't control ourselves there. Whatever the humans are doing under the influence of the magic doesn't faze anything, not when we can do damage a hundred times worse than that."

Leo gives him a nod, magic engulfing his body before Zoltan is finished talking. His body contours and twists, and in no time at all a large wolf shakes his fur before baring his teeth. No matter how many times I've seen the Alpha in his animal form, it never ceases to amaze me that animal and male exist together as one. I can see both of them peering at me through his eyes.

A kindling warms my gut for a second, but it disappears so fast I think I imagine it.

I wish I can feel as one with the monstrosity inside me as the shifters do their animals.

The wolf pounces off his hind legs and blends with the trees so fast it's like he is just a streak through the air. Tenebris grumbles a frustrated sound, almost as if calling the alpha a show off. We look at each other before turning to see Soren staring toward the city with a troubled look on his androgynous face. My eyes travel down his stiffened shoulders, watching the tense muscles of his arm and the white knuckled grip he has on the football helmet.

"Soren?" My voice is barely above a whisper.

He doesn't look at me. Staying as he is, he sighs, and I follow his gaze to see lights twinkling before us. From up the hill where I parked the car, I can see most of the human city spreading across the valley. It's unfair how calm and beautiful it looks from here, especially because of the situation we are in.

"Now what?" I ask without looking away.

"Now we wait." Zoltan comes next to me but stays just out of touch.

Good thing, too, because I'm not sure I want to be touched at the moment. My nerves are frayed, my chest is tight enough that I can't take a full breath, and I feel so fragile I think I will break if the slightest breeze blows.

"I never thought it'd come to this," Soren murmurs, and the blood curdles in my veins.

My mouth opens but no words come out.

"You knew someone crossed the portal and was stealing the book." Zoltan's voice is lacking the accusation I want to hurl at the ancient Fae.

Soren says nothing.

"And you didn't stop them," Astara hisses.

"I did not." A line forms between his eyebrows.

Something inside me breaks and I jump at him. All I can see is red, and the only thought in my head is to kill the fucker who, because of his stupid decision, has cost us many lives, including our own. Fangs bared, claws burst from my fingertips as my body sails through the air. Soren doesn't move, nor is he trying to defend himself.

Strong arms snatch me around the waist and rough fingers press hard on the side of my neck. Every curse word I can think of comes to the tip of my tongue to scream at Zoltan so he knows exactly how I feel about his interference, but darkness consumes me and I know nothing more.

Chapter Eighteen

Sitting in Myst's house, I keep staring at Soren and imagining all the different ways I'm going to kill him the second Zoltan slips. That's all I need, just one distraction and the Fae's head will be rolling across the floor. Myst found us in the forest and dragged us here saying Leo will come when he sorts things out back at the academy. Or so I was told.

How she knows what's happening across the portal is beyond me, but I wasn't in the state to argue. Being unconscious can do that to a female, especially with a stubborn ass like Zoltan around. It irks me more that the three of them and Tenebris act as if what Soren did is not a big deal. All I can think about is, if he knew this, what else did he know about and didn't lift a finger to stop?

Could he have stopped me from killing my brother?

"You need to let him explain, love," Zoltan murmurs in my ear, his cheek nuzzling on mine. He's had me pinned under him what feels like forever, pissing me off.

I jerk my head to the side and snap my jaws to bite him

like I'm some kind of feral animal, but he moves away too fast. Chuckling, the vampire shakes his head before stealing a quick kiss. When I glare at him, his smirk only widens.

"You should worry more about why Leo is not back yet and less about that traitor." Hissing through clenched teeth, I wiggle, but he is too heavy to push away. "It's because of him that we are stuck here under this bubble of protection like fish in a fucking aquarium."

"If I can trust you not to do something rash, I would go and check myself." I hate when he uses a reasonable tone with me. "Since that's not an option, I have to stay here and play peacekeeper." Pulling back so he can look at my face better, the expression on his softens. "Leo is a powerful alpha, love. And he is a member of the Order now. He will be fine. I'm more worried about whoever stands in his way."

"It's been two days." Grinning at him, which is more like me baring my teeth than anything humorous, I try to goad him. "How long do you think you can hold me like this?"

"Being on top of you, you mean?" Hunger sparkles in his blue eyes, and of course my stupid, traitorous heartbeat speeds up. "I can do this for a century or two." Winking, the corners of his lips slowly stretch into a predatory smile.

"If I have to listen to the two of you for another day, I'm going to scratch my eyes out." Myst saunters in from the front door, slamming it shut.

A harsh rap on the wood follows.

Craning my neck, I try to see what she's doing, catching her shoulders and head just as she turns to yank the door open. Myst stumbles back when Fenrir storms inside, my friends face twisted in anger.

"Oh, I forgot you were right behind me." Myst turns innocent eyes on Fenrir.

"I see why the two of you get along so well," Zoltan mumbles, watching the two of them stand at the entrance glaring at each other.

"Seriously?" His gaze falls on me, one eyebrow cocking up. "I've never made you chase me on foot while I'm driving a car."

"I'm sure that's only because you can't go through the gates. If you can go to Sienna, I'll have the same fate."

Rolling my eyes at him only makes him look at me as if I've proven his point. He is wrong. I've never done it, but that's only because I didn't think of it. I'll have to talk to Myst to get some ideas since Zoltan loves being an ass.

"Feumaidh sinn an ceàrr a rinn mi a rèiteachadh, rìoghail òg." Soren speaks and all of us turn to see him.

Lifting off the armchair he was using, the ancient Fae has eyes only for Fenrir. All the humor and mischief is missing from his expression, and that makes him look strange. Foreign even.

"English," I snap at him just because I can't help myself.

Inclining his head in my direction, Soren keeps his gaze averted away from me. "We must fix my wrongdoings. I requested assistance from the young royal."

"First you must tell us what else you did before you ask for help." My body jerks under Zoltan, my need to stand up and face Soren tugging at me, but my attempt is to no avail.. "Let's start with that, huh?"

"Francesca," Zoltan says my name in warning.

"Don't Francesca me." Turning on him, my voice grows louder with each word coming from my mouth. "How many people died while he played possum? How many more will die while he is brooding and feeling sorry for himself?"

"She has a right to her anger." Soren silences whatever

the vampire was about to throw back at me. "And she has a reason." I don't miss the glint in his gaze, though I still narrow my eyes on him.

"I guess all your crap finally caught up with you, Soren." Myst shoulders her way past Fenrir to stand above my head. I hate being pinned on the ground so my teeth grind audibly. "Let her up, jerk. I won't allow her to kill him. Your cock will shrivel before you get any after pulling this stunt, even though it's for a good cause. Am I right, Chicca?" She nods her head as if agreeing with herself and with the word vomit spilling from her mouth.

"As I said," Soren answers Myst on a sigh, "I've done wrongs. I would very much like to absolve myself. No matter if it was well meant, teine air a bhreith." A small smile plays on his lips and, to my shock, he bows at her. His head doesn't go below shoulder height, but even that from the arrogant Dragon Blood is too much.

"What did you call her?" It takes me a moment to realize Zoltan is off me and pulling me up along with him. It's the shock from seeing Soren bow, I swear.

"Fire born," the vampire answers me, still holding my hand while frowning at Myst, who has gone pale.

I move fast. Tenebris, who was curled up in a sunny patch on the floor, pounces just as fast, and everyone else tenses to stop me. There is no way anything can stand in my way, though. I need to reach the ancient Fae so I can scratch his eyes out with my fingers, which are curled into claws. I just want to see him bleed.

I want to see him hurt for what he has done.

The way I'm hurting.

Myst steps in front of me to block my view of Soren. The look of surprise on his face at the thought of being protected by her almost makes me laugh, but my "Oh,

Shit!" moment stops me in my tracks. Power slams me in the chest and sends me on my ass. The two-foot five female that speaks with no filter—and I'd like to say is my friend—transforms from one blink to the other.

A silver crown sits on top of her head, red stones glistening like blood encrusted on it. The same runes I saw on Fenrir swirl everywhere her skin is exposed. Her brown eyes are pitch black like the bottom of an abyss tugging at my soul. With her right hand extended toward me, she stands firm with her legs shoulder-width apart, her presence overwhelming.

My magic bursts out and propels me on my feet. I face her, my fangs bared while claws glint on the tips of my fingertips. Dizziness makes me sway, probably from standing up so suddenly, so I pay it no attention. The creature inside me that was taking a nap while Zoltan had his body draped over mine—and the bitch was purring, too—perks up. Emotions slam into me from her, to protect her, to keep her safe. My own are at war with it because she is in my way.

"Stand down, cousin." Her voice is not her own. This is the second time she's called me cousin, and I still don't understand why. "Nothing happens without a reason, and the web of life twists and turns to lead us to our fates. Do not take life unless you are prepared to offer one in return. I shall not stand in your way if you are willing to pay the price."

"I already paid the price with my brother's life that *he* could've prevented." Sliding to the right so I can sidestep her, she moves with me.

"But are you willing to pay with your own?" Her power hits me again, and this time it pushes me a step back.

Zoltan snarls and surges to attack her, but Fenrir tackles him to the ground.

"If he can kill me, then yes."

I send my magic at Myst but it only moves the strands of her hair. The strength I put behind it is more a thought than an actual action. It's almost as if I don't want to hurt her, or maybe I can't It's not like she's hurting me either, but it's pissing me off. That's when she delivers the blow that makes me deflate like a balloon.

"Think! His life is tied to Sienna. If you do kill him, which I believe he will welcome with open arms, are you ready to take his place?"

Both Soren and I hiss as if burnt at the same time.

Zoltan and Fenrir stop struggling, too.

Only Tenebris is watching with interest, not moving from his place in the sunlight.

"I will not leave her to that fate," Soren snarls at Myst.

"Not her exactly, no." Tilting her head, she gives me a slow, appeasing look before pointing a finger at my crotch. I glare at her. "Can you say the same about what she carries in her womb?"

This time I drop on my ass because my legs give out from under me.

Chapter Nineteen

Everyone starts shouting at the same time so they can be heard over the others. Zoltan scoops me up as if all of a sudden I have become an invalid and can't walk on my own, Dazed, I allow it, the cacophony of sounds, snarls, and growls lulling me into an out of body existence where I'm drifting between clouds with no feelings or emotions at all. Myst's words haunt me there, repeating on a loop.

"Can you say the same about what she carries in her womb?"

The smug feeling coming from the creature inside me strokes the kindling fire in my chest. I know I'm going to lose my shit eventually, but as of now, all I can do is blink and breathe.

The door opens and closes, more voices joining the yelling. Words like "fates," "destinies," "mistakes," "fights," and more drift to my ears, but nothing sticks long enough to make sense of it. Until I hear someone say, "Titans." Protective instincts blast like an inferno inside me and I scissor my legs, jerking out of Zoltan's arms. There is no magic behind my reaction. It's not like all of a sudden I can feel a life growing inside me. But knowing that there is ...

It changes everything.

Zoltan reaches for me and I slap his hand.

"Stop that shit." Glaring at him, I look around to see Astara and Daren. Leo has also arrived.

They stayed at the woods because they claimed their connection to the alpha didn't allow them to be so far apart. Or so Zoltan told me anyway. Seeing me watching him, Leo offers a small smile. It doesn't reach his eyes.

"The same magic is covering Sienna. It's a mad house back at the academy but we have it under control ... for now." Blowing out a breath, his gaze drops to my stomach. "I knew there was something different about you, but I never thought ..." Nostrils flaring, he shakes his head.

I look down to see my hand pressed on my stomach, and I snatch it away while heat creeps into my cheeks.

"Myst is full of shit." Not even I believe the words, but I say them anyway. "Soren told us that it was a possibility only a couple of days ago. That's not how that happens."

"Because unless you know it's an option it won't take, huh?" Astara giggles but stifles it fast when I turn a sharp look her way.

Zoltan's hand comes at me again, and again I slap it away.

"That would explain the explosion of power when the hunters attacked the other day." Daren is looking much better than the last time I saw him when he got out of the car at the woods. Everyone is nodding like that explains a lot of things.

"Wanna share with the new kid in the class?" Folding both arms across my chest, I stare him down.

"You control your actions and powers as long as the

youngling is not in any danger." Daren turns thoughtful, his eyes darting left and right as if trying to remember facts. "When it's in danger, your Dragon Blood pushes all rational thought out the door and acts on pure maternal instinct alone. Remove all threat at any cost."

"And you know this how?"

"You don't need to be a genius, Franky." The old Daren I knew comes out in the familiar smile and tone of his voice. "Regardless, if it's just a bloodline and not a shifter gene, a dragon is an animal. A scary and a very powerful one at that. It's logic, plus it makes sense."

"It does?"

"Of course. Zoltan has been unbearable to deal with, too, even more than usual," Leo says, while the others, including Soren, nod.

"Zoltan is always an ass." The said ass smirks at me, using the distraction to tug me to him. "As you can see. A stubborn ass, as well." Rubbing the back of my neck, I decide it's time to change the subject before reality hits me for real. Who knows what I'll do if I panic?

Ignorance is bliss.

Turning to Myst, I wave a hand around my head. "Where is your ..."

The female is back to her usual self, no sign of spooky eyes, glowing runes, or spiky crowns.

"You can see it?" The color blanches from her face, which earns me a scowl from Fenrir.

"Can't you?" I ask her stupidly.

"Of course I can. You're not supposed to," she snaps, and Zoltan growls at her.

"Oh look, we have two Neanderthals. Wanna see them in a fight? I'll bet you a serpentine stone mine will be the victor. He bites." Grinning like a fool, I wiggle my eyebrows, and it makes her laugh. "The winner keeps the stone."

"Speaking of which, you owe me one." She extends her hand palm up.

Sticking my hand in my pocket, I pull out the chain and let the stone drop in the air, dangling. Every eye in the room follows the movement, but I place it in her hand and Myst tucks it between her boobs without batting an eye. I had to carry the damn thing around with me because everyone else's reaction to it scared the shit out if me the first time they saw it. The power of that little rock turned them all greedy and acting unlike themselves. I'm glad to be rid of it.

"You have effective tactics to stop bloodshed," I tell her as I wearily move to plop on the sofa. Zoltan is next to me in a flash, pulling me under his arm like we are glued at the hip. "Not that I don't want to kill him for letting things get this far."

"It would be deserved, young dragon." It soothes me to hear the apologetic tone in Soren's voice. "I have failed you." I still want to scratch his eyes out.

"Someone mentioned a Titan earlier." The energy in the room turns gloomy as soon as I utter the word.

"We checked the book." Leo sighs, swallowing thickly. "You were right, Drake. Pages are missing in it."

"But Myst said the magic in this city started two days before we arrived. The timing is not right," I point out.

"The seals could've been broken if the child-god used your blood to tamper with it," Soren explains, absently scratching between his pecks as if trying to remove an ache. "With the invocations written in the book, it wouldn't take much at all to blast them open and release whoever was held by them."

"Are you saying we have a Titan to worry about on top

of Roberti?" Stomach churning, I press a hand on it so I don't puke.

Zoltan's hand goes on top of mine, and when I try to shove him away, he growls deep in his throat. At my raised eyebrow, his smirk returns. I snort. This shit is going to get old really fast.

"That's exactly what this magic comes from." There is no doubt in Soren's claim. "I dare hope I am mistaken, albeit on this, I am not."

"I'm still very angry at you," I tell the ancient Fae, who has the decency to look ashamed. "Your selfishness allowed you to look away when innocent people lost their lives. I want to know if we can count on you to help with this." His mouth opens, but I keep talking, not wanting to hear whatever bullshit comes out of him. "No more games, Soren. No more tricks and manipulation. Too much is at stake."

"My kind has very powerful seers," the ancient Fae muses, and we all watch him like he's lost his mind. Chuckling, he smiles like he knows a secret the rest of us are not privy of. "We lived our lives based on prophecies and told fortunes."

"I don't get it." Deadpanning, I narrow my gaze on him. "I said no more games and puzzles."

"No games, young dragon. Just the simple truth." He sighs and the sadness I see on his face guts me. "I was told a prophecy for my own fate one day. It made me want to end my life."

"Unfortunately here you are, fucking up our lives." Myst glares at me when I say the words, which tells me I'm really being an ass.

"That is deserved as well," Soren allows. "I didn't end my existence, as you all know already. I chose to wait instead."

"For the Titan?" Astara chirps, receiving a glare of her own from Myst.

That female really is very temperamental. An hour ago she hated Soren, now this. Go figure.

"No." A chill rushes up my spine when Soren's eyes lock on mine, intense and brimming with power. "For my mate."

"Oh, fuck to the no." Jumping up, I startle Tenebris, who has chosen to ignore us all. The panther hisses angrily jumping to his feet, too. "First you force Fenrir into a fake bond. Then you tell me my bond with Zoltan is a true mate bond, and now I'm your mate? You are crazy, old one."

"You are not my mate," Soren says calmly.

"Now you don't even know what you are talking about."

"Oh, dear fates." Astara breathes, pressing both hands over her mouth as her eyes brim with tears.

"Huh?" Confused, I look around at all the faces in various degrees of shock, and in Zoltan's case anger.

"An offspring from the last female Dragon Blood and a royal, a couple of millennia away. That is what the seer said," Soren says softly, his own eyes shimmering. "I mistook which royal was the true mate."

My knees buckle but Zoltan stops me from dropping on the sofa, gently lowering me in his lap. Lost for words, all I can do is stare at Soren. The ancient Fae stares back unblinking, allowing me to see all that he has suffered in hopes of seeing whatever story that seer told him come true.

"That's why you agreed to tie your life to Sienna? To feed an entire land with your own lifeforce?" My chest is so tight I feel like my ribs will snap in half.

"It's a small price to pay, young dragon."

"You really are crazy," I blurt out.

"Just honest." The corner of his lips curls up for a second. "A small price indeed if the alternative is loneliness for all of eternity." Those old, knowing eyes turn to Zoltan. "Wouldn't you agree, Zoltan?"

The vampire nods, tightening his hold on me.

I have a lump the size of my fist stuck in my throat.

"You could've told us the truth from the start." I have to clear my throat twice before I can talk.

"Would you have believed me?" Cocking his head to the side, he looks honestly curious.

"Probably not." My shrug is more of a jerk of the shoulder. "Even now it sounds like a sci fi movie."

"A what?"

"Never mind." Scrubbing a hand over my face, I blow out a breath. "Let's deal with the clusterfuck first. We can talk about mates later."

"I will help," Myst chirps, scratching at her arm. I watch her for a second longer to see that she's not scratching but tugging gently on a bracelet I've never noticed before.

"We. We will help," Fenrir corrects her, and she rolls her eyes.

"Do we know how to defeat a Titan?" Just saying it pools dread in the pit of my stomach. "I'd like to get my hands on Roberti, but I have no desire to deal with that crap."

"I'm sure between all of us, we can come up with a good strategy." Soren turns to the others for confirmation, which he gets. Especially from the males.

"We just need to find Roberti," I remind them, because we have absolutely no clue where he is.

"Not necessarily." Leo shuffles his feet uncomfortably.

"Meaning?"

"I think he will be trying to get across the portal sooner than we think." The alpha locks gazes with me, chilling my blood. "There was a message for you left inside the book."

"What kind of message." Ice is freezing my insides. Not even the heat from Zoltan's body next to mine can warm me.

Leo pulls a piece of paper from his pocket and hands it out to me. With trembling hands, I unfold it and the breath gets stuck in my lungs. The words Roberti said to me when he tricked me into taking the mission for investigating Daywalker Academy stare back at me in his cursive writing, all sharp lines and angry loops.

Drake,
I told you if you screw this up, you won't be getting out of there alive.
You screwed up.

Chapter Twenty

I'm not sure how to feel anymore.

Everyone is in a rush preparing for the inevitable. It's almost like they think if they run around enough they'll somehow prevent it. Zoltan and Fenrir have joined forces, and they are barking orders left and right in preparation of a war. My friends have their heads close together in what I assume is a meeting of the Order members, their heated debate being done in hushed, sharp tones and exchanged, meaningful looks. Only Tenebris and Soren don't look like they are in a hurry. The panther stays stretched out, his head pressed on his folded front paws as he pays attention to everything happening with a watchful gaze, while the ancient Fae does his best to pretend he is not keeping an eye on me.

"I do not envy you, Chicca." Myst bumps her shoulder on my arm.

"You stopped me from going after, Soren." Sighing, I give her a sideways glance. "If I fought him, no one would've said anything. You wouldn't have dropped the bomb, either, out of fear that you'd be next. Who wants to anger a female with blood on her hands?"

"True." I see her rubbing her fingers over the bracelet around her wrist. "How was I to know that none of the idiots put two and two together and figured out that you were preggo? One look at you and I knew, and that was before I got a whiff of your scent or your magic."

"You think they knew?" I narrow my eyes at Zoltan, who is listening to everything we are saying but is pretending he is paying attention to Fenrir. I know he hears me because his shoulders stiffen and his jaw tilts up stubbornly.

"Who knows about the rest of them? Soren and your hot piece of ass hunk, however ... I would bet my life on it." Myst gives the vampire, who is now glaring at her, a wide grin.

Now that she mentions it, Zoltan has been clingier than his usual stalkerish self lately. It's not like he doesn't know that I act rash and do stupid things that endanger my life, but he normally grumbles or tries to put me in an invisible cage claiming it's for my own good. Now, however, he has been more hands on, frustrated to no end with everything I do. Like claiming he will kill me himself if I run into situations like the one with the lashing magic coming from the portal. Or threatening everyone in the infirmary until they allow him to drag me to his room to recover there. I've woken up in his bed after being injured more times than after having sex with him. When the vampire is content it's easy to sneak out for a few hours, at least until he finds me.

He *always* finds me.

"I can't worry about it now." I look pointedly at Zoltan to make sure he knows I'll get back to it after this clusterfuck is over. If we are still alive, that is. "If anyone has a clue on how to kill anything around here, it's you." Turning my attention to Myst, I lock eyes with her. "You said it yourself that the humans are getting worse. We need to stop this now before it's too late." Taking a deep breath, I blow it out slowly. "How do you kill a Titan?"

"Chicca—" Myst starts, but the vampire speaks over her.

"You will not be killing anything." In his right mind, Zoltan slices his hand and chops the air, indicating there's no room for arguments.

Myst groans, slapping her forehead.

"And who is going to stop me?" Giving him a sweet smile, I blink my lashes innocently at the jerk. "You?"

"Francesca." That one word is said in such a condescending tone that it makes me want to scream.

"If you say think of the babe, I am going to kill you right here, right now." The growl coming from me shocks everyone in the room.

Soren snickers like an idiot before full-on laughing when Zoltan turns all his anger at him.

"You are old, Zoltan." The Dragon Blood grins as if he just told us the best joke ever. "Yet, you are so foolish." Shoulders shaking, Soren smooths a hand over his hair, eyeing the vampire shrewdly. "Have you no knowledge of dragons at all? As she is right now, not even I stand a chance against her. Females especially, even with distant bloodlines like ours, are the most aggressive when they are carrying offspring. She will rip us all apart if we stand between her and whatever she has set her sights on. Be it a sparkling jewel ... or a Titan."

"She." Jabbing a finger at my chest, I scowl at him. "Is right here. How about we don't talk about *she* while she can hear us, huh?"

"You have lost your ever-loving mind if you think I will allow my mate to face a Titan while carrying my youngling." Snarling, Zoltan takes a step forward, but Fenrir grabs him by the upper arm to hold him back.

Peals of laughter burst out of me, bringing tears to my eyes. "I'm sorry." Gasping for air and unable to stop laughing, I swipe the moisture from my eyelashes. "I thought you said *allow*."

Fenrir's grin grows while he tries, and miserably fails, not to look at Zoltan.

"Watch and learn." Myst swings a finger between me and the vampire.

Fenrir frowns, his face darkening.

"Anyway …" Unwilling to listen to drama between Myst and Fenrir, I puff up my cheeks, blowing the air out slowly as a few more giggles escape. "Let's focus less on Francesca and what she is doing, because she will be kicking some ass, and concentrate more on how the said ass is going to be kicked, shall we?"

"You will not stop her," Soren chirps, unfazed by the growing tension in the room. "You might as well have her as ready as she will ever be." Sucking in a breath, his nostrils flare and he keeps the sly look trained on a furious Zoltan. "For what it's worth, I have a vested interest to keep her alive, too. She will not go unprotected. I'd like to think that between the two of us she'll be as safe as can be."

Whatever Zoltan is about to say, which seems like a lot judging by the amount of air expanding his chest, is left unsaid when Myst stiffens, and after exchanging a fast look with Fenrir, they both run to the front door. Twisting around, I crane my neck to see what they are doing when Myst yanks the door open, closing it in the same breath.

Turning, she leans her back on it, her eyes flicking between all of us.

"You might not want Franky in this fight, Zoltan. Unfortunately, Roberti has other plans." Her gaze falls on me and stays there. "You really are a lot of trouble, Chicca."

"I'm not trouble. Trouble just finds me," I mumble under my breath, which earns me one of her rare, genuine smiles. "What? It's true."

"Simple is boring, never forget that." With a wink, her gentle expression changes into a determined one. "We have a crapload of hunters surrounding the house." Looking around the room, her lips twist in a grimace before she turns a calculating gaze on Fenrir. "It was about time for this place to go. The neighborhood was getting sketchy anyway."

"I bought the house across the street," Fenrir explains when he notices my confusion.

"Why?" As if that's important right now, but I can't help myself. These two really are entertaining. More so than Zoltan and me.

"She wouldn't talk to me." Shrugging as if he bought her flowers and not the house across from hers, he smirks. "Hard to ignore me when you have to see me all day, every day."

The daylight started disappearing a few hours ago, changing the bright rays to shades of burnt orange and pinks streaming through the windows. Even the darkening skies can't hide the shadows we see moving through the sheer curtains draped over the glass. Pushing off the sofa, I climb to my feet and move closer to the center of the room. Knowing these idiots, they'll start throwing the damn weapons when we least expect it. I wondered why when I stayed here not long ago, but I can see why Myst doesn't have a coffee table. The female is always prepared for an attack.

Tenebris uncurls from the floor lazily, his jaw opening impossibly wide in a yawn. Keeping one eye open on me at all times, I think his lack of sleep is finally catching up with him. Softly padding on the floor, he comes to my side, his tail snaking the only indication that he is agitated about being surrounded. Zoltan and Soren are on either side of me at the same time.

"This really is going to get old fast." Breathing the words gets the panther's attention, and he narrows his gaze at the two males. "You can bite them later," I inform him, and he perks. The shifter is a good friend like that.

The door bursts open, wooden shards flying like shrapnel all around us. Fenrir tackles Myst a second before Zoltan snatches me around the waist and spins me away from being impaled. That would've seriously sucked. The tickle of warmth in my bely blasts my insides like an inferno, and the view changes the same instant. It comes alive as colors dance and swirl, bright and dark cords leading my eyes to every living thing in and out of the house.

Grinning like an idiot, I jab Zoltan in the ribs.

"I know where all of them are." I'm practically bouncing in my excitement, but he watches me like I've finally lost it. Twirling my hand to indicate my eyes, which I know have changed, I keep poking him. My actions earn me a glare. "What if I burn them to ash…—"

The widow explodes inside, tiny pieces of it slicing my face and arms. With a hiss I duck, pulling Zoltan down with me as the rest drop on their knees and scatter like bugs to take cover. I don't think I've gotten braver because I still worry about the abominations trying to kill us. But it's strange to feel excitement instead of fear in a situation like this. The hunters always make me uneasy.

Well, they used to anyway.

Myst and Fenrir disappear through the broken door, and that's when the screams start. It's fortunate that the human city is insane from the magic Roberti released. Good luck explaining this if it happens at normal times. Another Purge waiting to happen to be sure.

"I see them as well," Soren calls out from behind me, and that's all the encouragement I need.

Crawling on hands and knees, I head straight for the entrance where I can unleash the building fire inside me. Zoltan and Tenebris are close enough behind me that they bump my ass with each forward movement. The panther slinks around me fast and is first out the door. Jumping to my feet, I'm next to him in an instant.

A hand grabs my braid and I'm yanked back just in time to avoid a dagger passing an inch from my nose. My eyes cross to see it, but it hurls so fast it imbeds the inside wall. I feel a hunter approaching behind Zoltan, so turning my shoulders, I duck under his arm, sidestepping to protect his back. The hunter's eyes widen a second before my claws burst out and slash at his throat. Deep red blood drenches his white uniform, making it look brown in the dying light.

With a ferocious roar, Tenebris pounces on the hunters coming at us from around the house. Releasing my braid, Zoltan joins him but doesn't move too far away from me. That's when Soren comes outside exiting the house like a tornado of a half-naked male and a waterfall of platinum hair.

The ancient Fae really needs a shirt.

Screams continue reaching my ears from the back of the house where I guess Myst and Fenrir are fighting.

Astara, Leo in his wolf form, and Daren rush to help, each of them wielding their powers much better than before. Bodies start piling up like broken dolls on the lawn, creating a macabre display ready for the day of the dead the humans love to celebrate.

We are making good progress, and just as the thought occurs to me that I won't need to release the burning magic inside me, the screeching of tires snaps my head to the right. Down the street I see them coming, dozens of SUV's approaching so fast they'll be on us in a second.

"This doesn't feel right." Tensing, I turn to face them just as Myst dashes from around the house, her hair wild and the silver crown gleaming eerily on top of her head.

"It's a distraction." Skidding to a stop next to me, she grabs my arm. "I could be talking out of my ass, but I know. I just know this is all to keep you here."

"Yeah, it does feel fishy, doesn't it?" The cars are almost upon us. "Roberti never sends a second wave of minions like this."

"You need to get back to Sienna."

A shiver passes up and down my spine, her words sounding more like a premonition than advice. A purr gets louder until the bike Zoltan used to bait me to come back home squeals to a stop with Fenrir straddling it.

"Go." Myst shoves my shoulder, and it makes me stumble. "Go!" she shouts in my face. "The two of us can handle this."

I want to argue, but something tells me that she is right. I do need to get back to Sienna, especially with both Soren and me on the other side of the portal. This is bad.

Really, really bad.

"We got this, cousin." With a firm nod, the cocky female is replaced by a formidable one who's ready to level the worlds. "Let us show them what we are made of. Bathe the earth with their blood."

Ignoring the goosebumps that sprout over my skin, I turn and run to the bike. Fenrir steps away when I jump on it, Zoltan making the metal groan when he settles behind me. Revving the engine, I glance at Soren and Tenebris, but they bolt down the street zooming past the incoming cars. Astara, Daren, and Leo are right on their heels on foot.

"I will see you later, Myst." Yelling at her back, I make her stop and look over her shoulder.

"If the Fates will it, you will." Her lips curl at the corners, and her expression tightens my chest. "Now go fuck them up." And she is gone in an instant right along with Fenrir.

"Fuck them up." Blowing out a breath, I get a good grip on the bike. "Right."

Throttling the machine between my thighs spikes up my heartbeat, and I bolt down the street past the hunters spilling from the cars like an arrow with Zoltan's arms wrapped around my waist.

Chapter Twenty-One

Wind blasts across my face hard, forcing me to keep my eyes narrowed to slits. The city zooms by in a blur as I weave through the streets, leaning down so low with each turn that my knee brushes the asphalt. It's been a while since I've had a bike. Mine was turned into scraps of metal somewhere between the gates of the academy and their front doors.

This too feels like a trail, only this time it's not just my life hanging in the balance. Sienna itself, with all its inhabitants, will either be left standing come morning, or …

I nip that thought in the butt.

The others must know shortcuts or something because I don't see them anywhere. Guided by the pull of magic the portal has on me, I follow its call like it's a siren song. The last faint rays of the day dip behind the horizon, brightening the glare of the light from the bike, which dances in front of us like a flashlight. The night that comes awake is different.

The darkness has a bite.

Clenching my jaw, I ride faster, fear that Zoltan will

succumb to the rage-filled magic making me feel as if we are standing still even though I can barely see from the speed. Whooshing wind fills my ears and prevents any other sound from reaching me. It's because of that that I don't hear the battle until we skid to a stop a lot further in the woods than if we'd used a car. The back wheel slides sideways when I brake, the momentum throwing me forward.

Zoltan releases his hold on me at the same time I let go of the handles of the bike and, tucking my head down, I somersault through the air, dropping on one knee. I hear the thump of his boots when he lands like a cat on his feet next to me. The clinking of metal on metal, roars, and screams greet us, all coming from between the thick curtain of trees. But that's nothing compared to the whispers brushing against my skin promising pain like I've never imagined. I glance at Zoltan to see him looking down at me, his eyes glowing brightly in the night.

"Can you hear it?" My voice is barely above a whisper.

He nods.

Just a sharp jerk of his head, but it says so much.

"Okay," I breathe, climbing to my feet. I brush the dirt from my hands off on my pants. "We got this, right?" Looking over my shoulder, I see the twisted handlebars of the bike, which ended up half nailed to a tree trunk. Wrinkling my nose, I peer at Zoltan again. "I broke this one, too."

"Just don't get hurt." His bright eyes drop to my stomach and my heart plummets to my feet. "I'll buy you a hundred of them each year to wreck and won't say a word about it."

"I'll remind you of this." Stabbing a finger at his face, I can breathe easier when one side of his lips curls up in a smirk.

"I'm counting on it, love." I'll never understand why his deep voice does stupid things to my brain, even when our lives are in danger. But somehow, I am usually turned into a puddle of goo when he's around.

Dumb, dumb hormones.

"Stay close to me. The energy does not feel right around here." Pinned under his scrutinizing gaze, it's me who simply nods now.

It'll do me no good to tell him I have no intention of staying close to anyone. Roberti has been hell bent on getting his hands on me almost from the start, and when that didn't work, he tried everything he possibly could to kill me. Now that I'm hoping to finally face him, I'll be damned if I let him kill those I love. Keeping my thoughts from showing on my face, I scan the woods and ignore Zoltan staring at the side of my face like he is trying to read my mind. I keep my emotions in check too, not letting him feel anything I'm planning through our bond. I hope he can't, anyway.

When he cups my face, I nuzzle his palm, placing a soft kiss at the center of it before stepping away. "Promise me …"

His eyes narrow and a muscle twitches on one side of his jaw.

I blow out a frustrated breath.

"Promise me that you'll make sure I come back to myself." Wiping my sweaty palms on my pants, I roll my shoulders. "I'm going to give this monster inside me full reign, Zoltan." Locking gazes, I try for a smile that freaks him out. "I want to be myself when this is over. I'm selfish, and I don't like to share you. Not even with a different part of myself." A sheepish shrug jerks my shoulder up like I'm having a seizure.

"I don't want you different," the vampire says just as softly, pulling me to his chest and tilting my face up with a finger curled under my chin. "I'll always be just yours, love."

"Good, I'd hate to have to kill you." He cringes. I guess the humor I am trying for is lacking. "Plus, I'll need you to take care of our babe." The whispered words try to choke me, but I push them out anyway.

Eyes shimmering with moisture he will deny as long as he lives, he kisses the life out of me. When he pulls back, I'm left breathless, sagging against him because my knees are weak and can't hold my weight.

"For as long as my heart beats, I will take care of you both." The possessive way he holds me would irk me normally, but this time it spreads warmth through my chest.

"You didn't have a heartbeat not long ago," I remind him, and the smile on his face is blinding.

"You gave it back to me." Packing a kiss on the tip of my nose, he winks. "Now you have to deal with it, love, for eternity."

That has the opposite effect than what he intended, reminding me of what's waiting for us across the dense trees. Hitching a thumb in that direction, I detangle myself from his arms.

"First, we need to kill a jerk." Swallowing my trepidation, I bring back my bravado. "And a Titan. Easy peasy."

Like a switch has been flipped, Zoltan grows in size, switching forms from one blink to the next. The unchecked power rolling off him prickles my skin, and that makes my own surge to the surface. Claws sprout from my fingertips without conscious thought. The creature inside of me comes awake, stretching out and filling my skin. It still feels too tight for both of us to share the same body, but the moment I let go of my control, it almost feels like this is how

I should be. The panic trying to choke me is squished when Zoltan laces his own clawed fingers through mine.

"Let's join the freak show." Flashing my fangs, I release his hand and move through the trees with a lot more grace than I'm normally capable of.

No sound comes from our footsteps as we reach the last line before the wide-open space holding the portal. It's familiar magic glides over me, welcoming and warm. A second later, arctic winds blast across my face, turning my eyelashes into icicles. Between one step and the next my teeth are chattering, and my fingers feel numb from the cold. Zoltan grabs my arm, yanking me back when I'm about to step out from the cover of the forest.

That's when I see it.

A Titan.

The evil creature is tearing through people like a cannon ball, sending limbs showering the open the space. Terror rolls off of it, blustering and coating my skin, choking me with it. I watch as it feeds off the fear and anger from those trying to stop it from reaching Sienna. My heart skips a beat when I see it heading for my friends, but I lose visual before seeing if they noticed it.

Standing next to Zoltan's true form I look like a teenager walking with a parent. The monstrosity trying to get to the portal at the moment makes me look like a two-year-old youngling. Power is rolling off him like a tsunami blistering my skin from the freezing cold air coming with it. At ten feet tall, the Titan's shoulders are as wide as a brick house, his arms and legs thicker than the huge trees hiding me from view. Deep red skin stretches across a muscular frame, his body naked other than the loincloth hanging low on his hips. He swings his gigantic fists, flinging those trying to stop him from reaching the portal away as if they are toys. Dozens of hunters are helping him, attacking viciously at anything standing in their way.

And then there is Roberti.

I'll recognize that asshole anywhere.

Aware I can never win against the Titan on my own, I pick the lesser evil. If I'm going to die I'm taking the jerk with me. With Casius next to him and another mage I've never seen before, they stand just to the side of Andrius, using magic to break the protection of the portal. From where I'm standing, I can still see the horrifying shadow writhing behind him reaching for the two mages as if feeding on the magic they use. They must not be able to see it. No one in their right mind will stand next to that.

"If we take out Roberti, will that affect the Titan?" Instead of stepping out to be seen, I move along the tree line just out of sight, and Zoltan follows close behind me.

"Titans have nothing anchoring them to this world in this day and age. It'll need an anchor to be physically here and be that powerful," the Daywalker murmurs, not taking his eyes off the monster.

"Andrius used himself as an anchor." We are nearly halfway around the tree line, getting closer to the demigod. "That must be the shadow attached to him. It feeds off his greed and makes the Titan able to absorb the life force from everything around him. Now I understand why the colors feel drawn to him. It didn't make sense before."

"What shadow?" Taking a fistful of my shirt, he prevents me from going further.

"You can't see it?" Looking over my shoulder, he shakes his head, both eyebrows pulled down his forehead. "It's attached to him just like a typical shadow, only this one is not on the ground. It's alive and moving like a cape around him, feeding off the magic from the two idiots standing next to him." I shiver visibly.

"If we remove the source of his food and the anchor, he should be easy to take out." I've never heard Zoltan sound so unsure. "I can take those three on my own."

"You can't even see the shadow." My voice is so dry I expect to have clouds of dust coming from my lips.

"Stay close to me." His jaw clenches in warning, but I roll my eyes and tug my shirt from his grip.

"Let's kick their ass."

"Francesca."

"You finally get to play my knight, Zoltan. Go kill the Titan, I've got Roberti."

Leaving Zoltan's angry hiss behind, I bounce off the balls of my feet and take hold of a high branch above my head. Like the monkey I love referencing myself to, I swing from branch to branch, closing the distance between Roberti and me faster than Zoltan can move on the ground. Leaving all thoughts of how pissed off he will be later if we survive behind, I let my magic wash over me and pull me under. Reaching a thick trunk right across from the demigod, I pause for just a second before sailing through the air. My body resembling a cannonball, I drop a few feet from Roberti.

"Hey asshole, I believe it's me you are hoping to find in Sienna." His head snaps in my direction. "Surprise!"

Chapter Twenty-Two

"Drake, I thought you were smarter than this," Roberti drawls, his frosty glare so full of hatred you'd think I killed his puppy.

I hear Astara's voice from somewhere between the fighting bodies but can't tell if she's calling out to me or just yelling at someone. At least I know they're here, which only adds to my ever-growing list of things to worry about. Tenebris roars, his cry rising above the rest of the animalistic snarls. I keep my gaze locked on Andrius, even when Zoltan dashes past me and hits Cassius in the back, both of them rolling to the side with fists flying. It's a bad move because the shadow writhing behind Roberti seems like it started paying attention to me.

"I am smarter. That's why I'm here to end this once and for all." The purr in my voice added by my Dragon Blood has Andrius raising an eyebrow as he looks me up and down.

His dark eyes glitter with glee when they zoom in on my stomach.

I clench my fists.

How is it that everyone can tell I'm pregnant and I had no clue? Isn't it like an agreement between your body and mind to kind of inform you of it before it broadcasts it to the world? I feel like my body has betrayed me.

"I sacrificed a lot of my hunters to keep you away from here." Spitting the words like I should apologize for killing his mutants, he bares his teeth.

"Aww, next thing you'll say is you were trying to protect me. Am I right?" Keeping an eye on the fight between Zoltan and Casius in case I need to jump in, I slide my feet closer to Roberti and hope he doesn't notice. "You want nothing more than to see me die. I'm always happy to disappoint you."

"That's where you are wrong." We both stumble when the freaking Titan stomps his foot, trying to shake off a pack of wolves nipping on it. "I would've made the biggest mistake had I managed to kill you in my attempts. Alexius was an idiot. He would've cost me much if you didn't get him out of my way."

"That's me, always happy to help a friend." Seeing that he starts circling me, I stop hiding my steps and move along with him. "Now I'll kill your two buddies, and you. You can thank me later, it's fine, I can wait."

"Always feisty." Chuckling, he pisses me off when he grins like we are out for a stroll. "I always liked that about you, Drake."

"Why are you doing this?" clenching my fists, I stare him down. "You spent years trying to keep the Accord alive. We all looked up to you. What in the worlds are you trying to achieve when you had everything. Especially power, if that's what you are after."

"That's exactly the problem, Drake." Spitting the words

as if he tasted something vile, Roberti's face twists in a terri-fyingly ugly grimace. "Are you telling me it pleases you to jump every time a human sneezes? Oh, you thought I wasn't aware of that little leash you have, were you?" his chuckle is crazed. "We must obey human laws. A prey telling a predator how to walk the jungle. Humans don't even have that in fairytales. I'll be damned if I allow them to collar me and have it in real life."

"And you what? Figured you'll destroy us all to teach the humans a lesson?" snarling at him, my knees bend slightly preparing to take a chance the moment I see an opening. "I should've known it's something stupid like this."

"I am a god." His voice booms, the echo bouncing all around us. "I will not tilt my neck in submission to my food. The Titan is just a toy until I get what I want. If you are smart, you'll join the winning side while you have time."

"You want more than just a Titan?" ducking my head I peer at him, my reaction making him glare at me.

"I will bring Ares to his rightful place in these worlds, his army will be ready and willing to do anything he demands. And I will rule by his side as is my birthright."

"I won't let you do any of it, Andrius. Say goodbye to your dumb plans, because this ends right here, right now."

"For this to stop, I will need to die." He acts confident enough, anyone else would've believed it.

Pouncing without warning, I swipe my claws at him, one at his neck and the other at his midsection. He spins, kicking out and catching me on the side of my thigh. I rake my claws across his stomach, leaving rips in his button-down shirt that is getting soaked in blood.

We both stumble away from each other.

"Less talking, more dying." Grinding my teeth, I ignore

the throbbing in my leg and the fire the pain sparked in my chest.

It's not time yet.

I have a feeling I'll only have one shot to take him out.

"I'm not going to kill you, Franky." The familiar way he says my nickname makes me shudder in revulsion. "I have bigger"—His eyes flick to my stomach again—"better plans for you now."

The female creature that attacked me a few days ago comes to mind and blinding fury surges through my veins. I don't need Andrius to spell it out for me. I know exactly what his bigger, better plans are. There is no doubt in my mind the second he realized I was with young, he lost interest in my death because I carried in me what he is attempting to create with his experiments. No, he doesn't want me dead.

He wants my young.

My shoulders hunch and pain sears through all my bones. For a moment I fully expect my skin to burst open and a dragon to appear to stomp Andrius into a bloody pulp. My jaw and gums are burning like someone is pulling my teeth one by one very slowly, and I taste my own blood on my tongue. An insane thought blinks through my head that if I'm not shifting, maybe I'm having a heart attack. Wouldn't that be a bitch to be recorded in history as the one who died before getting a chance to fight.

My body is shaking like I'm having a seizure and my claws sink into my palms where I clench my fists so I don't cry out in pain.

That's when Roberti strikes, like the snake he is.

A fist connects with the side of my face shattering my cheekbone. Head flinging to the side, I go down but my body never hits the blood-drenched ground. Arms catch me, lifting me in the air and dropping me behind a wide, muscular back. The long black hair sways down to his hips as Zoltan stands like a shield between Andrius and me.

The asshole demigod is rubbing his chin, blood trickling from his split lip. I guess the Daywalker scored a good punch before stopping my fall. Grinding my teeth while my face burns from my healing cheekbone, I place a hand on Zoltan's back. He grumbles something but presses on my palm like he needed the contact as well.

"Love?" His deep voice vibrates through my palm.

"I'm fine." The words are not out of my mouth yet when another wave of the searing pain hits me, bowing my shoulders. "I lied. I think I'm dying."

"Francesca." Zoltan doesn't take his eyes off Roberti, but there is no mistaking the panic in that one word.

At least Roberti is not attacking. Instead he's warily watching us both.

A ball of magic zings from the side, hitting Zoltan and grazing the arm I have connected to his skin. He screams, a pained and furious sound that provokes a reaction in me I don't expect. The pain turns blinding for a second before my spine snaps back and I find myself staring at the starless sky.

A roar curdles my blood, making the ground at my feet shake like an earthquake.

Everyone turns to where we are facing off, including the Titan.

The roar comes from me.

Blanching, Roberti spins on his heel ready to bolt just as my head snaps back up. I'm on him before I become aware that I've moved, my claws sinking into his back and raking chunks of his skin with each swipe. He jerks his hips to the side, flipping me off him, but I bounce back on my feet throwing myself at him again. His hands wrap around my wrists to hold the sharp claws away from his face. While we struggle, the ground trembles beneath us, and Zoltan starts cursing up a storm.

A red haze covers my vision.

Everything is bathed in the color of blood.

Headbutting Andrius is satisfying, but stars burst behind my closed eyelids from the impact. The shadow, which stayed out of our fight until now, uses that distraction to latch onto me, the feeling of slimy magic pushing bile to the back of my throat. It's tentative at first, but as soon as I notice the pull of magic from my body, the horrible thing visibly shudders and redoubles its efforts. The ground is quaking harder too, making it seem like we are on a boat. The world around us is swaying.

Zoltan's foot comes into view as he kicks Andrius in the face, barely missing mine by an inch. I had every intention of using my fangs on the jerk, but luckily the vampire reacted faster than me. Roberti's head flings to the side, his grip on my wrists loosening. Instead of rolling away from him, I try to rip his throat out, but the rocking of the earth jerks me forward and my claws sink into the hard, packed dirt.

I'm plucked off Roberti and thrown aside just as a huge shadow falls over the spot where I was standing only a second ago. Landing on my hands and knees, I crane my neck to see the Titan glaring down at me, his eyes literal flames burning on his ugly distorted face.

I bare my fangs at him.

The Titan stumbles, almost falling to the side.

My heart skips a beat in excitement before I see Soren flinging magic at the monster, running toward us like the hounds of hell are on his ass. Platinum hair streams behind him like a white waving flag, but the expression on his face is terrifying. Tenebris is pounding the ground with his giant paws while he moves around the ancient Fae. From the corner of my eye, I see Zoltan pounce and sink his claws into the Titan's ribs. The creature swings his arm to fling him away, but the vampire ducks and shreds every inch of skin he can find.

There is no graceful movements or calculated hits. Something primal is awake in Zoltan, and he snarls while cleaving his way across the monster's body. Soren joins him, taking a long jump and attaching himself on the Titan's chest. When they take him down on his back, Tenebris is on top of him too.

It opens the view of the portal where the mage I don't know is still pushing magic like his life depends on it. Astara and Leo are trying to stop him by combining their powers. Sprawled on the ground at the mage's feet is the dead body of Cassius.

Zoltan's pained shout jerks my gaze away from my friends, and I see the Titan tightening his hand around the vampire's throat while swinging at Soren and Tenebris with the other keeping them at bay. Lost in the sight, I don't see Roberti moving until he grabs hold of my hair and yanks my head back. A dagger is pressed to my throat and the stench of poison clogs my nostrils.

Back off," he barks loud enough to be heard by everyone. "Or she dies."

I try to push him away, but the blade bites into my skin and warmth spreads down my neck. Zoltan stops struggling and goes limp in the Titan's hold. Soren and Tenebris slink back, watching Roberti with trepidation. Even Astara and Leo release the magic fighting the idiot that is doing his best to open the portal. The mage says something shrill in a language I don't understand, and Roberti grinds his teeth.

"I might die, but I will kill you before I take my last breath," I snarl at Roberti.

"I said stop, Daren," Andrius shouts, and I finally see my friend standing too close to the portal, the swirling lights hiding his position. Magic is streaming from his hands and blocking the asshole who is trying to open the gate to Sienna. Swaying on his feet, Daren looks like he is about to shrivel into a husk, but he doesn't stop his assault.

"I said stop, or ..." Roberti growls.

With a menacing grin, he slides the dagger from my neck and presses it against my lower belly. The breath freezes in my throat, my lungs shriveling from lack of oxygen. The deadly point of the blade sinks into my skin just enough to prevent me from moving. Everyone is frozen as if they're holding their breath.

"I will carve the abomination from her stomach while she is still alive," the demigod announces with too much glee in his voice.

Zoltan's scream brings tears burning the back of my eyes, but I don't dare blink. Holding my breath, I beg Daren silently in my mind not to listen. My mind is spinning. What can I do to avoid what I see as an inevitable fate? Even if I blast him with my power, he will have enough time to sink the blade into my womb.

"Daren," Zoltan roars my friend's name, his voice promising him hell if he doesn't listen.

My eyes dart to Soren and the defeated look on his face breaks my heart, regardless of the fact that I'm angry at him for being a manipulative ass. I flick my eyes to Daren, whose skin is turning gray and his lips are blue, cracked, and bleeding. My heart stops beating when his arms lower slightly.

No! Don't stop!

I scream at him in my head, but I can tell he is about to give up.

"Which would you save, Drake?" Roberti gloats, jabbing the dagger deeper. "Your mongrel, or your friend? Either way I'll have what I want. There is nothing you can do about it."

That kindling that I kept feeling in my belly turns into a blinding fury trying to consume me. My skin turns blistering hot, which forces Roberti to hiss even though he doesn't let go. There is a gasp from someone, but I only have eyes for the fucker trying to kill my young.

It all happens so fast.

Tucking my hips in, I tug the dagger out, twisting my hips and nailing myself on it until the tip of the blade embeds itself in my hipbone. Roberti's eyes pop out so wide they'll fall out of their sockets any second. With a feral grin, I open my jaw wide and strike at his throat. Fangs sinking into soft skin, I literally chew through his neck, the gushing blood spraying all over my face. Screams and shouts turn into white noise until his head falls off his shoulders, the shadow blinking out of existence. Good thing he was arrogant enough to hold it back. He thought he had me where he wanted me. I did tell him many times that would be his downfall. When I'm left with his headless body in my arms, I start clawing at it.

I don't stop until there is nothing but a mush of broken bones and handfuls of grinded muscle on the forest floor. When there is nothing left of him to destroy, I lift my head, blinking the blood out of my eyes. The hunters are dead, there is no sign of the Titan, and everyone is watching me

—some with fear and others gawking like idiots. Licking my lips, I lock eyes with Zoltan, who looks like he wants to scoop me up and is afraid to approach me at the same time.

"I told him I would kill him," I rasp through a raw throat.

"That you did, love." Approaching cautiously, he reaches for me, leaving his hand palm up for me to decide if I want to take it.

When I try to move, I flinch, the dagger hurting like a bitch sticking from my hip. Zoltan's eyes fall on it and he forgets to be wary. Dropping on his knees, his hands hover over the hilt because he's too afraid to touch it.

"Soren," the vampire barks, and the ancient Fae is next to us in a second. "It stinks like poison."

"It's Titan blood," Soren spits in disgust.

"If I turn ugly like that jerk just kill me," I tell them, faintly swaying on my knees.

"Nothing will happen to either of you." The Dragon Blood takes hold of the dagger with one hand while pressing his other wrist to my lips. "Take it, young dragon. I give it freely … for your young."

My gaze flicks to Zoltan, and he clenches his jaw but nods once.

I sink my fangs in Soren's wrist.

Everything is a haze of loud voices arguing and flames trying to melt my insides. When all the pain stops and I can hear myself think, I find Zoltan, Soren, Astara, and Leo looking down at me, with Tenebris lying on the forest floor next to me, his head pressed to my arm.

"Daren?" I don't want to ask, but I have to know.

Zoltan shakes his head and a tear slides down my face, which is followed by many others that soak the collar of my bloodied shirt. I'll always regret that I never told him I forgave him. Out of all of them, he knew me the best and did what I wanted him to do like he could read my mind.

"It's finally over." My voice cracks, but I don't care. All of them are shining because of my glossy eyes.

"Indeed, it is." Soren looks like he wants to reach for my stomach,

I kill his temptation by taking Zoltan's hand and placing it there for the first time.

"She is okay." I've never seen that many emotions playing across Zoltan's face. If I'm not mistaken, he looks like he is about to faint.

"She?" He swallows thickly, his gaze darting from his hand on my stomach to my face.

I make sure he sees me look pointedly at Soren. "Yes she, unless the old fart swings the other way."

Zoltan barks out a laugh.

"Now take me home." Lifting both hands, I urge him to pick me up.

"You want me to carry you?" His eyebrows crawl to his hairline.

"Yup. I'm going to milk this shit for all it's worth. No more walking. You'll carry me around like a personal mule."

Shaking his head, Zoltan curls me to his chest and stands.

"You too, Soren." I wait until the Dragon Blood is on his feet to give him a wicked grin. "I'm going to make you my bitch until this youngling is old enough to come to your defense."

I've never seen the ancient Fae so pale.

Daren, my brother, and many others will be missed and mourned for years to come. I'll make it my mission for everyone to remember their names. As Zoltan nears the portal preparing to lead us home, I look over his shoulder to see Leo staying behind. His gaze connects with mine and I know without asking that he is not coming back with us.

"The Fates have other plans for the alpha," Soren murmurs when he spots who I'm looking at.

"I think you are right," I tell him.

Leo's shoulders slump, but he nods in gratitude when he hears my words. Then he disappears into the trees.

Maybe now I can finally get some sleep.

Also by Maya Daniels

vinci-books.com/blackhand

They made me their weapon. Now, I'm aiming at them.

The Council spent a thousand years crafting the perfect assassin—
me. I played along... until they killed my friend. Now? I'm taking
them down one body at a time. With a vampire, a human, and a
shifter at my side, the Council's reign is about to end. They won't
see this coming.

Turn the page for a free preview...

Black Hand: Chapter One

I was unprepared.

I wasn't ready for the curve ball life was about to throw at me.

Nor did I anticipate what the fates had in store for the near future.

The tiny pinpricks of light reflected through the window of the plane, the city below the metal bird stretching over the hills as far as I could see. I mushed my face closer to get a better look, but the glass fogged from my breath. My stomach dropped when we lost altitude, the winds lashing at the plane making the last fifty minutes of the flight turbulent and unsettling. If it went down, it'd solve a lot of my problems. Although …

I was unprepared for that, as well.

I wanted to live.

My heart skipped a beat when the light blinked on above my head for the seatbelt, the loud chime echoing through my head like a gong going off. The plane was made for humans, not creatures like me with super-sensitive hearing. Being an *Atua* was seen as fiction in this world. They liked to call us vampires, but little did they know we were very much real, we lived among them, we manipulated their lives for our gain, and we had no remorse at all. Well, most of my kind didn't. I, on the other hand, was cursed ... or something. I cared a little too much.

I should've expected my reaction to get attention, but I did not. It would've saved me a lot of hassle if I didn't flinch like a rookie. Too late I noticed the flight attendant beelining my way with a look of determination on her face. Her hands were swinging by her body in fast, sharp jerks as her legs scrunched her skirt above her knees from her long strides. The woman was on a mission and there was no mistaking that.

You'd think she was about to fight a crocodile to save my life.

"You doing okay there, doll?" Her brown gaze locked on my face, the expression there telling me I'd better not lie to her, and her hairstyle with not a single hair out of line said, "Don't mess with me.".

"I'm good, thank you." Offering a small smile that was more a press of my lips than anything else, I stared at her chin. A bad habit I'd developed through the years so I could keep my eyes hidden. They gave away the fire scorching my insides from the anger I'd internalized for centuries. To humans they were just freaky, I guessed.

"She gets nervous when flying," Veronica chirped from next to me, shifting in her seat and flipping her blonde ponytail over her shoulder with a delicate hand. "She'll be fine as soon as we land."

"We are almost there." The Flight attendant gave me a

once over as if checking for tells that I wasn't being truthful. "Keep your seats up and put your seatbelts on. Around this time of the year, the winds don't make it easy for those that get jittery on a flight."

"Will do," we both piped in with tight smiles aimed at the attendant, and I turned to look out the window again because I was done talking. I heard her footsteps slowly walking away after about a minute, and she'd probably stared at the back of my head that whole time.

"Stay alert. You're slipping," Veronica murmured under her breath, her words too low for anyone but me to hear her. "Snap out of it before we have the same situation we had three years ago."

"Right." Ignoring her jab about my trip to the cages— where I spent an entire year in darkness with barely any blood to keep me alive—I kept my eyes glued to the glass, seeing nothing, though her words did send a ping straight through my gut. My fingers trailed over the inside of my left forearm, the phantom pain reminding me of the ripped flesh that used to be there regardless of the smooth skin covering it now. The cruel voices laughing and gloating at my pain while they teared my flesh were trying to drown me, but I clenched my jaw and pushed them away. I would not dwell on that now.

Not ever.

Immortality was seen as a blessing by humans, their lives spent dreaming of having eternity to do everything they wanted. They envied creatures they read about in books, creatures like me that kept their youth and roamed through centuries. What they didn't see was the ugly truth behind what we were. They were blind to all the suffering we went through while our physical bodies stayed the same, only memories of the pain left behind haunting our dreams.

And there wasn't even a scar to show for it.

Only memories.

Snatching my hand away, I tightened my fist and used the sharp bite of my nails to bring me out of that dark hole filled with misery. Nothing good ever came from dwelling on the past. Yet ... darting my gaze across the lights below us, I couldn't help the sigh that escaped me. I wished I was down there with them. I wished I belonged to their world instead of the hellish nightmare mine was. It was difficult to swallow the lump clogging my throat while my lashes fluttered to get rid of the burn behind my eyes. I would not cry. Looking back, I hadn't cried for years, and I had no intention to start now. No, I had a job to do.

"You need to move," Veronica mumbled as she turned to face me, her brown eyes full of pity. My lips pressed in a firm line of displeasure, but I couldn't blame my friend for feeling sorry for me. I was an emotional, pathetic fool most days, and what I was sent here to do would be just another thing to add to my nightmares. "Don't do anything stupid, Brooklyn, I beg of you. Not now."

A lock of fire-red hair fell over my eye and I blew it up in frustration. It wasn't like I planned to do stupid things, though the word stupid was debatable depending which perspective one used to look at things, of course. I just had issues with blindly following orders. Personally, I couldn't say needing more information before you took someone's life was stupid, but what did I know? According to those that ruled over my life, not much obviously.

"Bee?" Veronica squeezed my knee and brought me back to the present. "I can do it—"

"No, I got this." I didn't allow her to finish the sentence. She had done enough to cover for my little rebellions. I handled the cages. Veronica wouldn't last a week.

Plus, I had a plan.

A stupid one, of course.

"Forty minutes until landing," my friend reminded me, staring over the seat in front of her as she flattened invisible wrinkles on her pencil skirt.

Leave it to Veronica to be dressed to the nines no matter the situation. The black skirt she wore was paired with a silky champaign colored blouse that complimented her pale skin and blonde hair. With six-inch heels and her long legs folded primly to the side, she was ready to be on the cover of a magazine, not in an economy seat on a flight to Chicago. Or next to someone like me who was covered from head to toe in black leather, including the boots covering my feet. My fire-red hair and eerily bright green eyes were the only color anyone would ever see on me. I liked my clothing to match my mood, and it had been as dark as it could get for so long I couldn't remember it ever being any different.

My body jerked forward when one of the children sitting behind me kicked at the back of my seat, throwing another tantrum when his mother told him to put his seat-belt on. The poor woman was hissing threats at the boy, but they did nothing to intimidate the kid, though her voice was trembling from either her need to cry or just plain anger, but I had no clue which. Blowing out a breath through pursed lips, I nudged Veronica so she would let me out, pretending I didn't see the old pervert across the aisle ogling her ass when she gracefully unfolded her body like a swan rising from sleep.

She reached her arms up, stretching and twisting slightly left and right, which always did the trick. There was not one person on the plane that didn't stare openmouthed at her beauty. As far as distractions went, I couldn't ask for a better one. Sliding out of my window seat and keeping my eyes in front of me, I headed out to the lavatories separating us from the business class. Veronica's drowsy *"Oops, oh dear, I think I'm dizzy"* was drowned by the rustling of clothing when everyone jumped out to help, including the two flight attendants who were practically running to come to her aid.

My feet kept moving forward.

The red curtain wavered slightly as if someone was moving behind it just as I neared the door of the bathroom I was pretending I wanted to use. The plane dipped and we lost altitude again, but my steps didn't slow nor did my balance suffer from it. If anyone noticed, I wasn't aware of them. I kept getting closer to my goal. *You can do this. There is nothing to fear,* I reminded myself just as I reached for the curtain.

The thick fabric was yanked back before I touched it.

"You are not fine." It was the same flight attendant from earlier, her eyes narrowed on me in suspicion as she gripped the curtain in a tight-knuckled fist.

I didn't slow down.

My boots ate up the space between us, and she took a step back as if startled by my advance while she filled her lungs with air like she was about to tell me off or maybe even scream. Using my speed, I was next to her before she had time to process what was happening. I covered her mouth with one hand while pulling the curtain closed with the other. Left in the tight confines between the metal drawers behind her and me in front of her, her eyes bugged out, her nostrils flaring as she panted in fear. Lowering my face to hers, I allowed my lips to curl just enough so she could see the tips of my fangs. Her heart was hammering so hard I could feel it under my palm on her face. Such fragile creatures, humans were.

"Sleep," I whispered, taking hold of her upper arm when her eyes rolled to the back of her head.

Not a great plan, but it'd have to do. By the time she woke, she wouldn't remember what was reality and what was a dream. A perk no one but Veronica knew I had. Compelling people with your voice was a myth from human stories, and it was one that everyone laughed about.

I didn't laugh about it.

I was hiding it so I could keep my life.

Loosing precious time, I placed the woman in one of the seats in the tight place designated for the flight attendants before straightening and staring at the second curtain that would take me to the business class.

A throat cleared from somewhere in front of it and paper crinkled when the page of a book was flipped over. Behind me voices were overlapping, and among them I heard Veronica's assurances that she was okay, but they weren't very convincing, even to me. The girl was good when putting on the charm.

I slid through the curtain, my gaze darting over the top of the chairs until it stopped on the third row. He looked just like the rest of the humans, apart from two things that made him stand out: his steady heartbeat and the way his sweaty palm gripped the hand rest a tad too tight. Also, the stench of a shifter seared the inside of my nose so much my eyes watered from it. Ignoring the curious glances from those I passed, I walked up to him and crouched next to his seat, pretending I knew him by placing a hand over his forearm.

"If you make any sudden moves, I will kill you before you have a chance to blink."

Smiling sweetly, I watched his eyes widen in shock before bulging in horror when he saw my fangs. His dark, terrified gaze dropped to the pendant nestled on my throat —a symbol that made me someone's property and that was the same red color as my hair—and I watched a drop of sweat slide down the temple of his blanched face. His body trembled with the need to stand up and attack. Broad shouldered and easily over six feet, he was a male in his prime left to quake in front of a female he could break in half if given a chance. Well, any other female but me, that was.

It broadened my smile.

"You will walk with me back there." I jerked my head to the side and pointed at the extended area where I left the flight attendant. "One wrong twitch of a muscle and this plane will land with only corpses occupying it. Yours will be among them."

He lifted a shaking hand, spearing his fingers through the mass of curls sitting on top of his head. The stench of the sweat that had his shirt sticking to his body was burning my nostrils, but he blinked fast a few times before swallowing thickly and nodding his head. There was no mistaking the defeat in his eyes. Pushing up, he stood at the same time as I lifted off my crouch, my head reaching just slightly above his shoulder. My cocked eyebrow was enough for him to sigh and get moving without trying his luck. There was a good reason I was sent after him. We both knew he couldn't win.

Not with a monster like me.

The moment we were both crammed in the tight confines, I yanked the curtain closed, the sound making him flinch and face me with his knees slightly bent. Ignoring his fear, I strained to hear if Veronica was still entertaining her audience, and my own knees buckled in relief when I heard her soft chuckle.

I startled the male by taking a fistful of his shirt and yanking his face close to mine. "Can you shift here?"

"Wha-what ..." he stuttered, but I didn't have time to wait for him to get his head out of his ass.

"Can you shift?" He kept gaping at me, so I shook him to get his brain online and glared at him. "The Syndicate is sending their regards, asshole. Will you shift, or will you die here?"

"I've done nothing ..." When a muscle jumped in my jaw, he shrunk back and pressed his back to the metal drawers. "I can shift." His gravelly voice shook, the confusion in his deep brown eyes almost comical. Only, there was nothing funny about the situation for either of us.

"I will need you to shift and stay in the cargo area with the rest of the animals on board until you are transferred to the unclaimed baggage. A human will come to claim you there and take you to a safe house where you will stay as long as it takes. For the rest of your life if need be, do you understand? If you don't, we are both as good as dead." When he heard he wasn't going to die tonight, he almost dropped on his knees as his legs gave out on him. I had to hold him up by the flimsy fabric of his shirt while he nodded with gusto. "Hey." Hissing under my breath, I jerked him upright. "Look at my face and remember it as good as you remember your own. The time will come when I will need a favor. I will find you and you will do what I ask. Am I clear?"

"Of course ... anything ... please ..."

"Shift."

I had to take a step back when he instantly obeyed, and between one breath and the next a gray wolf was pinning his ears while snarling at me where the male should've been. It tucked its tail when I bared my fangs at him. Keeping him in sight from the corner of my eye, I opened the latched door to the cargo area and he bolted down like his ass was on fire. I felt like my soul was in flames from the need to go down there and join him, too. Closing it, I stiffened for what I was about to do, but they left me no choice. I would not kill a creature like me just because they told me to do it. Not if I could help it.

Sticking my head out through the curtain, I crooked my finger at the first person who turned their head to see who was coming out. A human in his sixties with unassuming features, his receding hairline making the top of his head shine in the low light of the plane took the bait.

"Come." The human got up and joined me, keeping his watery blue eyes pinned on my face. *He doesn't have that much longer to live*, I convinced myself.

Acid burned the back of my throat.

"This will not hurt," I promised him as I closed the distance between us.

My shoulders were thrown back and my head lifted high when I joined Veronica back at our seats. Sliding in, I settled into my window seat, my distant and unseeing eyes looking through the glass. She shifted slightly next to me, that small movement speaking louder than if she shouted at me.

"It's done," I told the window, not daring to look at her.

A scream from ahead of us pierced the silent air of the plane, and it was followed by one of the flight attendants yelling for a doctor. Not that anyone could save the human now. My hand fisted in my lap.

"It had to be done." Veronica sighed, sinking back in her seat in relief.

"Yes." My heart did a painful pump against my ribs

once before resuming its natural slow rhythm. "Where the Syndicate is concerned ... this had to be done."

Good thing she had no idea what *this* was.

For both of our sakes, I'd make sure the Council never found out exactly what I had done either.

Grab your copy...
vinci-books.com/blackhand

About the Author

Maya Daniels, USA Today Bestselling and multi-award-winning supernatural suspense author, is a fun-loving woman with many talents.

She traveled the world, gaining life experiences that helped her career as an investigative journalist, as well as her storytelling. Maya writes compelling tales of magic, mythical creatures, loyalty, and life-changing friendships with snarky female characters—much like herself.

Her travels have taken her to Europe, Africa, Asia, Australia, and America. Born with her feet in motion, she currently resides in Ohio, spinning her next epic story that you will not want to put down.

Her biggest 'sins' are her love of chocolate and coffee—through an IV drip! One to never sit still, Maya practices Reiki healing, different types of martial arts, reads about the arcane, talks to furry creatures more than humans, picks up a sledgehammer for home improvement, and travels with her fated mate, seeking her own adventures.